VINCENT RUSSO

15-Love

First published by Vincent Russo 2025

This novel is entirely a work of fiction. The names, characters and incidents portrayed in it are the work of the author's imagination. Any resemblance to actual persons, living or dead, events or localities is entirely coincidental.

For permission requests, contact the author at: [www.vincentrussowrites.com].

First edition

ISBN: 979-8-218-78785-1

This book was professionally typeset on Reedsy. Find out more at reedsy.com

To my friends, family & chosen family. Thank you for always believing in me amidst my creative chaos.

Prologue

If I won, it wasn't just for me. That thought had looped through my mind a hundred times since the match began, now embedded in me like a reflex.

The umpire called play for the final set. I moved in a daze, barely aware of how I got there or who I was, even playing against

A few points slipped by in an instant. I trudged back to my side of the court and glanced at the scoreboard, trying to remember how to breathe. My legs wobbled like jelly.

The scoreboard read: WC Rion Miller USA 5−7, 4−6, 6−3, 7−5, 6−6, 5/3 (3rd seed) GRE Stefano Gonzalez—final set. I was up 5−3 in the tiebreak.

"Why do men's Grand Slam matches have to be best of five sets?" I muttered to no one. "Best of three would be so much easier."

I approached the baseline, aligning myself. I zoned in on the ball in Gonzalez's hand, bracing for the serve. My body screamed with exhaustion, but I blocked it out.

Gonzalez bounced the ball twice. Just as he tossed it up, a loud noise broke through the air.

Beep. Beep. Beep.

The chair umpire raised his hand and apologized for the technical glitch. Play resumed.

I felt my anxiety rise from my belly, in my chest, and in my throat. I held my breath as Gonzalez prepared to serve again.

And then time slowed. He tossed the ball high, leaped into motion, and smashed it toward me with blinding speed.

My eyes widened as the ball rocketed my way, but my reflexes—those beautiful reflexes—kicked in. I shifted left and met the ball with a clean hit, sending it straight into Gonzalez's racket.

He didn't hesitate. In an instant, he fired it back, and I was already sprinting forward, forcing my body to reach the approach shot.

I attacked with a sharp backhand. The ball skimmed the far corner line.

Everything went silent.

One beat. Two beats.

The crowd exploded into a roar. People leaped to their feet, cheering, and I had never felt so alive. My muscles tensed as I imagined a victory dance. I felt like I deserved it.

"Let's do this," I said to myself.

The score was 6–3. One more point. Everything came down to this. Strange, how everything I'd worked for hinged on this one moment.

Gonzalez looked furious, his nose flaring with every breath. It was intimidating, but I shoved the fear aside and sucked in a sharp breath, zeroing in on the ball gripped tightly in his beefy palm. His hand twitched. He was about to serve.

"You got this, Rion," I said under my breath.

He tossed the ball and drilled it toward me. It clipped the net and landed outside the service box, in the doubles alley.

A beginner's mistake. Good for me.

He pulled a ball from his pocket and served again, but something was off—it was coming in unusually slow. A mishit. I couldn't help the grin tugging at my face, and I unleashed a heavy forehand down the line.

But my joy didn't last. The ball clipped the net again.

I held my breath. Then luck stepped in. The ball bounced over to Gonzalez's side. Relief surged through me.

But it wasn't over.

Gonzalez sprinted forward and somehow got his racket under the ball, pushing it back over.

It was a floater. No spin.

The opportunity hit me like a surge of adrenaline. I lunged, energy surging through me. This was it.

I reached the ball in record time and sent a soft cross-court volley into the open court.

It landed perfectly square on the line.

The crowd went wild.

I dropped to the ground, overwhelmed. Emotions choked me. I did it. I did it. Tears pricked my eyes, annoying, but impossible to stop.

Beep. Beep. Beep.

I jerked awake, blinking against the flashing red lights at the edge of my vision.

The alarm shrieked in my ears. A half-smile tugged at my lips. I was dazed.

Wait... did I win this time

Chapter 1

It was the last day of summer vacation. Tomorrow, I'd be a sophomore.

First thought: *What should I wear?*

I stretched and glanced around my messy room, piles of clothes on the floor, posters of Serena and Venus Williams, Shawn Mendes, and Little Mix plastered on the walls.

Jesy, I still can't believe you left the band, I thought to myself, staring at the poster of Little Mix.

Spotting last night's dinner plate on my desk, I sighed. Better take it to the kitchen before it grows legs. I placed the dish and fork in the sink just as Mom called from the other room, "Have a good run, sweetie."

I called back, "Thanks, Mom. Go back to bed."

I headed down the hallway to change for my run, hopping over Luna like always. She barely lifted her head, gave a single huff, then flopped back down, clearly unbothered by my acrobatics. Luna was a four-year-old mutt we'd adopted two years ago, and in that time, she'd mastered the art of selective interest.

By 6:22 a.m., I was out the door. Forty-five minutes later, I was back and jumping in the shower. Sundays were my light workout days, just a quick run and done.

After drying off and getting dressed, I checked the clock. A little past 8:30. Mom's car was gone, she must've gone grocery shopping.

I threw together some cereal and yogurt, topped it with granola and honey-maple cinnamon. As I savored every spoonful, my phone vibrated and lit up with a text from Sarah.

"Hey, what's the plan for today? Last day of freedom before school starts again!" she joked.

I quickly responded, "Hey! No idea yet. Just finishing breakfast. What time do you wanna meet up?"

Almost immediately, she replied, "It's 8:30. I'm still in bed. Can we pretend you didn't wake up at a ridiculous hour on a Sunday to work out? Let's meet at Honey Hive around 1, when normal people are awake."

I grinned. She knew me too well.

The Honey Hive was our go-to, and the only café in town, unless you counted the Starbucks by the highway. But since neither Sarah nor I had a driver's license, we rarely went that far.

On the way there, I caught the usual glances and weird stares. People in town probably thought I was nuts. I couldn't help it— I always practiced a modified version of my forehand while I walked. It was all about making contact out in front. To everyone else, I probably looked like I was swatting at a fly.

As I turned onto Main Street, a bright cherry-red car whipped around the corner straight at me. I had to dive out of the way.

What the f—

The car screeched to a stop. The window rolled down, and a deep voice called out, "Don't be such a drama queen, Miller."

I didn't have to look. I already knew the voice.

Jason Banks.

"Ugh," as I got to my feet. "I'm fine. Thanks for checking."

Who even taught him how to drive?

Jason chuckled, flashing that devious grin I knew all too well.

"Later, Filler Miller," he called before speeding off down Main Street. You could hear the unmistakable banshee of a laugh that comes from only one person, Ashley Smith. If Jason was there, she wasn't far behind. Ashley was the Harley Quinn to Jason's Joker.

Charming as ever, I thought, shaking my head as I continued walking toward the café.

The sidewalks were mostly empty, just a few cars parked along the narrow street and the occasional breeze stirring the leaves. Main Street was quiet, like it always was on a Sunday afternoon. A few faded storefronts and chipped wooden signs lined the block, and the distant hum of lawnmowers buzzed through the air. Somewhere nearby, someone was grilling, it smelled like summer and charcoal.

By the time I reached the Honey Hive, it was a little after one. I pushed open the door, the old bell above it giving a soft jingle.

No sign of Sarah. I rolled my eyes. Typical.

How can the smartest girl in class always be running late?

The Honey Hive had that cozy, rustic charm I loved. Wooden tables, oversized couches, exposed brick walls, and local art and vintage photos of the town added a nostalgic touch. It was the perfect small-town spot.

I walked up to the counter, glancing at the menu even though I'd seen it a hundred times.

Without thinking, I mimicked my forehand again, swinging an invisible racket.

"Hey, Rion. Still working on that tennis swing?" I heard a voice on the other side of the counter.

At first, I smiled at the sound of the familiar voice, but then

6

my nerves kicked in. Did I look cool and relaxed? Or like a complete idiot?

I thought about my outfit. A black tee, blue jeans, a backward baseball cap, and the ratty old Converse I should've thrown away years ago.

Meh, I'd looked worse.

Trying to find the right words to say hi, I just grunted.

A loud voice from out of nowhere rang out from the window seat: "We'll have our usual—two iced honey vanilla lattes. Make mine with nonfat milk."

I glanced nervously at Shawn behind the counter. He chuckled, pushing a few loose strands of dark auburn hair behind his ear.

"Sounds like my sister strikes again. I'll bring those right over."

I reached for my wallet, but he waved it off like my money was no good here. Smiling, I walked over to Sarah's table and sat down.

Sarah sat sideways in the chair, dressed in her typical high-waisted jeans, a worn green graphic tee featuring a hand-drawn solar system, and a chunky knit cardigan that looked like it had seen better days. Her auburn hair was loosely gathered in a messy bun, with a pencil stabbed through it like a flag atop a hill. She absentmindedly spun her black-rimmed glasses with one hand while scrolling through her phone with the other.

"Ugh, sorry about Shawn. He can be such a pain sometimes," she said, rolling her eyes.

"No worries. He's great, I mean, fine. It's fine," I stammered.

Smooth, Rion. Real smooth.

Quickly changing the subject, I asked, "So, what's the plan for today?"

With her usual quick wit, she replied, "Well, I thought we could hang here for a bit, catch up, considering you were at that weird camp all summer. Then, we can head to my place. Mom's ordering pizza for dinner, and we can watch a movie."

Before I could remind her that weird camp was my summer job, I heard that same deep voice from behind us.

"Miller! If I knew you were coming here, you could've hitched a ride with me!"

Jason turned back to his table, laughing with his friends.

Just as I opened my mouth to respond, Ashley scoffed loud enough for the cafe to hear, "I bet that's his dream, being sandwiched in a car full of guys."

Classic Ashley, always trying to chime in after Jason. She had overly-straightened hazel-brown hair, cover-model looks, and the attitude to match.

We'd never been friends, but we'd crossed paths enough for me to know she was sharp, calculating, and always ready with a well-placed dig.

Before I could say anything, Sarah shot back, "Jason Banks, are we still on for tutoring tomorrow, or did you finally learn your ABCs?"

Laughter bubbled from Jason's table, but it died quickly when Ashley shot them a sharp look.

Smiling back, Jason said, "Oh, the more one-on-one time we spend together, the better."

Then, with a nod, he and his friends got up and headed out of the Honey Hive. As they walked out, Ashley yelled across the café, "Miller, I think there's a glitter cookie with your name on it at the counter!"

My face burned with embarrassment. I let out a sharp sigh and turned to Sarah.

"I hate that guy. Do you have to tutor him?"

Sarah shot me a quick, reassuring smile. "Just ignore him. Hottest guy in school, biggest jerk on the planet. But hey, his parents are paying me double, so joke's on him."

Shawn arrived with our lattes, setting the cups down in front of us. Sarah perked up, eyes bright.

"Thanks, Shawn. I think we need a slice of that honey lavender cake, too."

With a quick nod and a smile, he disappeared behind the counter to cut us a generous slice. The moment Shawn set it down, the sweet, floral aroma filled the air—so delicate it almost felt wrong to eat it.

With two lattes and a thick slice of cake between us, Sarah leaned in. "Now, where were we? Oh yeah, that weird camp. Tell me about it!"

I giggled and shook my head. "Sarah, it wasn't a weird camp. It was my first real job, and I wouldn't shut up about it before summer."

I'd been proud. It wasn't glamorous, but it was mine. And it paid enough to cover next year's tennis lessons.

Sarah nodded like she'd just remembered. "Right, right. So, how was it?"

I told her about teaching kids to swim, breaking up splash fights, and dealing with one camper who kept hiding flip-flops in the lifeguard shack. She laughed at that. I tried to stay focused, but when she started talking about her summer textbooks, AP prep, and some online bio course—I zoned out.

She was always like that. Driven. Smart. Laser-focused. I, on the other hand, was counting down the days until my next tennis match. I nodded while she talked, but my mind drifted to the court, where I felt most like myself.

By four p.m., we left the café and started walking to her house. We could've made it in twenty minutes if we rushed, but instead we strolled, letting the town pass by slowly.

Chapter 2

We didn't get to Sarah's house until five. Her street, lined with well-kept ranch-style homes and neatly trimmed hedges, always felt like a different world from mine. Kids zipped by on bikes, sprinkler arcs glistened in front of lawns, and there was a gentle hum of barbecues firing up in the distance.

Just as we reached her driveway, Shawn pulled in behind us, his beat-up Jeep kicking up a soft crunch of gravel.

He leaned out the window with a grin. "How'd it take you this long to walk home?"

Sarah rolled her eyes. "Ugh, shut up."

I couldn't help but giggle. There was something oddly comforting about how siblings could say so much with just a couple of words.

As we made our way up the driveway, Shawn called out again, "Mom! When are we ordering pizza? I'm jumping in the pool real quick."

A spark of nerves, or maybe something closer to excitement, zipped through my chest. The pool. It wasn't just the water that made my stomach flutter. It was Shawn. Even hearing his voice made my heart knock a little too hard against my ribs.

Sarah caught the look on my face and narrowed her eyes. "What's with you?"

Panic. I scrambled for an excuse. "Oh, uh... I just remembered my mom's doing a back-to-school dinner tonight."

Smooth, Rion. Real smooth.

Sarah raised an eyebrow but didn't press. "Aw, that's sweet of her," she said, softening. Then she smirked. "But now you owe me dinner for ditching me for your mom."

As I turned to leave, her voice followed: "And don't wear those old Converse tomorrow! They look like they've been run over by a truck. Repeatedly."

I smirked without turning around. "No promises."

By the time I got home, it was just past 5:30. Our cracked driveway led up to the familiar sight of Mom's faded silver sedan parked under the drooping maple tree. The screen door creaked as I stepped inside, and almost instantly, I heard her voice from the kitchen.

"How was tennis practice today?"

Before I could answer, she corrected herself. "Wait—Sunday. You went for a run, right? See, I pay attention."

I laughed, heading toward the fridge. "Yeah, you sure do."

Grabbing a water bottle, I made my way down the hall toward my room. Just as I reached for the doorknob, she called out again.

"Dinner will be ready in twenty minutes if you're hungry!"

I smiled to myself. *She has no idea I just used that as an excuse at Sarah's.* "Okay, great!" I called back.

"Oh, and Rion, I picked up a few things for you today. They're on your bed."

I stepped into my room and froze. Two overflowing shopping bags sat at the foot of my bed. Next to them, a small black shoebox, unmarked. I ignored the clothes and went straight for the box.

Inside: brand-new, all-white Converse All-Star high tops.

I let out a squeal and kicked off my old ones like they were on fire. The new ones slid on perfectly. I all but jogged over to my mirror, twisting to check out the view from every angle.

Still wearing the sneakers, I finally turned to the bags. Mom had gotten a little bit of everything—jeans, tees, a couple of button-downs. But as I sifted through it all, a pang of guilt surfaced.

How did she afford all this?

Before I could spiral too far, I heard her call from the kitchen. "Dinner!"

The moment I stepped in, the smell hit me, beef, cheese, onion, and pastry crust. I gasped.

"Cheeseburger pie?" I asked, almost accusingly.

Mom grinned, placing a warm slice on my plate. The golden crust cracked under the fork, revealing sizzling beef, melty cheddar, and the sweet pop of caramelized onions. I devoured it like I hadn't eaten in days.

"Okay," I said between bites, "this is dangerously good."

Mom rubbed her belly in fake sympathy. "You didn't seem to be complaining."

I leaned back in my chair and let out a dramatic belch. "My compliments to the chef."

She gave me a mock-glare. "Really, Rion?"

We both laughed. It felt good. Easy.

After dinner, we worked together to clear the table. While I dried the dishes, Mom glanced over and asked, "Are tennis tryouts coming up?"

I gave her a look. "Tryouts are in the spring. But I start lessons at the club later this week."

"Right," she said with a nod. "That's what I meant."

13

Once the last plate was stacked, she pulled the towel from my hands. "Go chill out or something. I've got the rest."

I didn't argue. I kissed her on the cheek and whispered, "I hate drying dishes."

Laughing, I bolted back to my room, already feeling lighter. I threw on my favorite Spotify playlist, Mom's Night Out, filled with '80s and '90s ballads, plus a few new gems from Lizzo, Bruno Mars, and Fifth Harmony.

I dove back into the shopping bags, laying everything out on the bed like a personal runway. Tomorrow was the first day of school, and somehow, even with everything else swirling in my life, I felt ready.

Chapter 3

I slowly opened my eyes and stretched my arms out wide. Yawning, I glanced at the alarm clock on my bedside table. It read 7:15 a.m. My eyes widened like saucers.

Crap! I'm going to be late for the first day of sophomore year!

I threw the blanket off and raced to the bathroom. In a blur, I splashed water on my face and swiped on deodorant, realizing too late it was Mom's ultra-sensitive Dove. Rolling my eyes at myself in the mirror, I swished some mouthwash and sprinted back to my room.

The perfect first day of school outfit hung on a hanger in my closet, but there was no time for perfection. Yesterday's jeans and a hoodie would have to be good enough. I yanked them on and bolted down the hallway. Running full speed, I tripped over my brand-new, still-untied Converse but somehow didn't fall. I burst into the kitchen like the house was on fire.

Mom whipped her neck around so fast, I swore she might've pulled something.

"Morning, Mom," I said, half out of breath. "Breakfast?"

She laughed. "Your breakfast is on the table."

I didn't wait for her to finish. I bolted to the table, where a glorious heap of waffles waited for me, alongside a tall glass of milk. My stomach growled, but I knew if I sat down to eat, I'd be even later.

"Can I take these to go?" I called, shoving a waffle into my mouth.

"This is not a fast-food restaurant, Rion. There are no to-go orders here."

I sighed dramatically, chewing fast. The milk was warm, but it helped wash the waffle down. I drained the glass and grabbed two more waffles, and ran out the front door.

As I climbed the steps of Olympia Heights High, that familiar weight of gloom hit me. My Converse slapped against the stone steps, loud in the early quiet. I glanced through the classroom windows, same desks, same stiff chairs. Nothing had changed.

The security guards. The teachers are waiting by the doors. The desks. The chairs. All the same, old and dull.

I bit my lip, that weird metallic taste creeping in. My feet moved faster toward the first period. As I stood outside the school, looking up and the weathered build, someone snuck up behind me and whispered.

"Hey, Miller."

With a quick jerk that nearly knocked me over, I realized I knew that voice.

I turned and saw the grinning eyes of Sarah.

I ran my fingers through my hair, trying to fix the mess. She stood there in ripped jeans, oversized sleeves, a tangle of necklaces, and her long hair spilling over her back. Thick black-rimmed glasses framed her usual smirk. And I suddenly had no idea what to say.

Sarah tilted her head. "You always stare at people like that, or am I just lucky?"

I blinked. "Sorry, I was trying to figure out if you joined a band or robbed a vintage store on your way here."

16

She laughed. "Jealousy doesn't look good on you, Miller."

"Neither does that sweater, but here we are."

She bumped my shoulder with hers. "Still got that big summer ego, huh?"

I grinned. "Only when I'm winning."

"Please," she said, walking ahead. "You nearly lost a water balloon fight to a toddler at that weird camp you went to this summer."

"Hey! That kid was ruthless."

She glanced back, smiling. "Come on. Homeroom starts soon."

Classes were a blur. Homeroom was basically a free period, and English II wasn't much better, our teacher was already building a reputation for being late. I used the time to scroll Instagram and zone out with my earbuds in, my mini mental escape on day one.

The rest of the day crawled. Everyone was busy showing off their first-day fits—new jeans, spotless Jordans, while I dragged around in old jeans and a hoodie that smelled like my mom's deodorant.

With the school day nearly over, it was time to start thinking about heading to the country club for my tennis lesson with Coach Moore.

The sun hung low, casting a warm glow over the tennis courts as I jogged to the service line, gripping my racket tightly. Coach Moore was already waiting near the net, and I caught his piercing blue eyes. His face, weathered by years of sun and stress, was creased with lines and shadowed by stubble. He was getting older, but there was no doubt he still had it.

Coach Moore wasn't just any coach—he was a former Division I college player with years of competitive experience. His reputation as the toughest coach at the club wasn't exaggerated. He'd trained some of the best players in the state, and I had only trained under him in group sessions before. But now it was just me, the court, and Coach Moore, watching my every move.

"Alright, Rion. Today's all about footwork. Stay low, light on your feet, and ready to explode," Coach called.

I side shuffled to the left and right, my sneakers squeaking as I lunged and sent the ball back with a solid pop. My legs burned as I moved, trying to stay sharp.

We moved on to forehand and backhand drills, followed by approach shots, and ended with volleys. My legs were on fire, sweat dripping down my back, but I pushed through.

Throughout practice, Coach roared, "Stay balanced!"

"Keep your head up!" he barked after a long forehand. I fought through the exhaustion, determined not to show any weakness.

As practice came to an end, Coach Moore approached me at the bench by the court.

"There's something else I need to talk to you about."

I looked up, suddenly alert.

"Lessons are going up," Coach said, his voice firm. "Starting next week, it's going to be $100 per session."

The number landed like a gut punch. I swallowed hard, trying not to show it.

"Today's still the old rate," he continued. "But I wanted to give you a heads-up. Prices are rising for everyone."

I didn't have words. I had no idea how I was going to pay the new lesson price.

"I... I understand," I said, my voice not quite steady.

Coach nodded, steady-eyed. "You've got talent. Stick with it, and you'll keep improving. You've come a long way in a short time."

"Alright," he added, clapping me on the shoulder. "Get some rest. We'll hit it hard again next time."

As he walked off and I packed up, the thought of losing those lessons sat like a rock in my gut. But for now, all I could do was focus on what I could control.

On the bus home, a tightness crawled into my chest. Everything, practice, money, just life, pressed down on me. What was I going to tell Mom? It already felt like we were scraping by.

When I finally got home, I burst through the front door and immediately yelled: "Mom! The club's raising its rates. Coach told me today!"

I dropped my bag on the couch and collapsed next to it, sinking into the cushions. I leaned back and closed my eyes, frustration pressing against my chest.

A soft whine snapped me out of it. Luna, tail wagging, waited at my feet. I picked her up and set her down in my lap, running my fingers through her fur.

"Hey, Luna," I said, rubbing her ear like I always did.

In the kitchen, Mom stood with an apron on, hands dusted in flour up to her elbows. Was she baking cookies again? She looked wiped, like she hadn't slept in a week. Even from the couch, I could see the purple shadows under her eyes.

Guilt punched me. Why did I blurt out the lesson hike?

Trying to recover, I switched gears. "What are you making, Mom?" She walked over, standing beside me with a blank expression.

19

"Did you say the club raised their rates?" she asked, voice tightening.

Crap. Crap. Crap. My attempt at distraction wasn't working.

"Uh... yeah," I said carefully, watching her closely. It was like I'd just knocked the wind out of her. She dropped onto the couch beside me, her face somber.

"We'll figure this out. We will, okay?" Her voice was soft, but it sounded like she was trying to convince herself more than me.

I gave a small nod, hoping her words weren't just something to say.

She reached out to ruffle my hair. I pulled away without thinking, and Luna jumped off my lap, startled. "You've got flour all over your hands, Mom," I said, forcing a chuckle as I gestured at her fingers.

Her absentminded "Oh!" made me wonder if the news was already weighing on her.

She caught me watching and tried to smile, but it didn't land. I could almost picture her with a sign around her neck: Smile temporarily out of order.

"I saved enough from my summer job to cover next month's lessons, so it's fine."

Her expression barely shifted.

She forced another weak smile and, with a full-body sigh, turned and went back to the kitchen.

Luna trailed after me as I headed to my room. The overpowering vanilla smell hit me the second I walked in. A few weeks ago, I'd tried masking the stench of sweaty gym clothes with Febreze instead of doing laundry. Then I tripped on a pile of clothes, and the bottle slipped from my hand, dumping all over the carpet. The smell never really left, no matter what I tried.

Now it just made my stomach twist. I'd give anything to get rid of it for good.

I wasn't trying to eavesdrop, but as I grabbed my doorknob, I heard Mom down the hall, talking low on the phone. She was definitely trying to keep her voice down, but I could still hear her.

I eased the door open and stepped inside. Luna bounded after me, yipping.

I froze. Mom was still talking. With a quiet breath, I crept down the steps. At the bottom, I paused again, listening. She sat at the kitchen table, back turned to us. Perfect.

"...financial strain right now. We can't afford the increase, even if I wanted to. I just—" Mom paused, listening. She shook her head, frustrated. "But Coach Moore, you know how much Rion wants to train. I want that for him. Please, if you could make an exception—"

She was cut off mid-sentence. Her face fell, the defeat so visible it made my chest ache. The thought of her begging my coach lit something in me. My fists clenched as heat crept up my neck.

The line went dead. She lowered the phone, staring at it like it had betrayed her. Then she turned and spotted me in the hallway, Luna pawing eagerly at my fingers. Her scowl landed hard.

"How many times have I told you not to eavesdrop on my conversations, Rion?"

"But Mom—" I stood, my voice louder than I meant. "I couldn't help it."

She opened her mouth, then paused, thinking.

"I could take another job," she said quietly. "Then I could cover the fees."

21

I stared at her. "You know I'm not letting you do that. I'd rather quit."

"But you—"

"Mom, no. I'm not letting you take another job for me." I looked at Luna. She glanced between us, sensing the tension. "C'mon, Luna."

We headed down the hallway to my room.

Luna jumped onto the bed and spun a few times before settling at the top of the bed.

I flopped down next to her. Her tail thumped as she waited for me to cuddle her.

"What do you think, Lu? Should I really let Mom take a second job just to cover my lessons?"

I rolled onto my stomach and started rubbing Luna's ear, and drifted off to

Chapter 4

I had never liked logarithms. Half the time, I couldn't even pronounce the word right. Just seeing them scrawled across the page made my brain short-circuit. Math gave me chills, the kind that crawled up your spine and settled behind your eyes.

And yet there I was, slumped across a mismatched wooden table at the Honey Hive Café, across from Sarah, who was chewing the cap of her pen like it held the answer to question two.

The Honey Hive had that cozy, rustic charm I loved. The windows gave a soft view of Main Street, quiet this time of day, where rust-colored leaves scraped across the sidewalk, and the occasional pick-up truck rumbled past.

Our notes were a disaster, crammed into dog-eared textbooks that looked like they'd survived two decades and a flood. I stared down at the mess and sighed.

I was good at tennis. I couldn't also be a math genius. That'd be too much for the world to handle.

I groaned, yawned, and started poking at the edge of the table with my pen.

Sarah looked up and snatched it out of my hand. "What are you doing?" she hissed, eyes darting toward the barista, who had just finished steaming a pitcher of milk behind the counter.

"What?" I leaned back in my chair, trying and failing to look innocent.

"Are you trying to destroy this table? You know how hard it is to find a seat here after four?"

I held up both hands like I was surrendering. "Wasn't on purpose. Sue me."

Sarah rubbed her eyes and let out a long breath. "What are we even doing here?"

She started laughing at first, just a chuckle, then a full, slightly unhinged giggle. I couldn't help but follow. Her laugh always pulled me in like a magnet.

In between breaths, she wheezed, "I'm completely blanking on question two. What do you have?"

I raised my fist to my mouth and belted out in falsetto, "I got youuuu, moonlight, you're my starlight..."

Sarah narrowed her eyes, trying to hold back a smile. She did that thing where she pretended I wasn't funny, even though she totally thought I was. Only best friends could see through each other like that.

"Why are you such a goofball, Rion Miller?"

I grinned. "I have no idea, Sarah Russell."

Then, without warning, someone shoved the back of my chair hard enough that I slammed into the table.

I whipped around.

Jason stood behind me, smirking like he'd just delivered the line of the century. He wore that same oversized varsity jacket, even though the weather didn't call for it. A few heads turned. The barista glanced up, then looked away. The café quieted, just enough to make my neck flush with heat.

"Back off, Jason," Sarah snapped, standing now. "Try picking on someone who can stoop to your level."

She always stepped in. Always had my back. And even though I appreciated it, part of me hated that I needed her to.

Frustration tightened my chest. I shoved my chair out and stood, ready to say something—anything—but Sarah reached over and touched my arm.

"Don't," she said, steady and calm. "He's not worth it."

I hesitated, chest rising, pulse quick, but sat back down.

"You look constipated," she added, smirking now. "Seriously. Your face is doing this... thing."

I scoffed and closed my books, dropping my chin into my hand.

"What's the point, Sarah? School feels pointless when all I care about is tennis. I just don't get it."

Sarah didn't skip a beat. "So, tennis. You started back at the country club, right?"

I exhaled through my nose, my shoulders sinking.

"Yeah, but I've only got enough saved for maybe a couple more lessons. The club raised its rates, and after this month, I'm out. I don't want to go back to YouTube tutorials. Those only got me so far. I told my mom, but it's like... every time we jump over one hurdle, there's another waiting. I just want things to be easy for once, you know?"

She rested her chin in her hand, mirroring me. "You're acting like the world's ending."

"Isn't it?" I mumbled.

She poked my forehead. "Rion. Your mom always figures something out. She's like, full-on scrappy genius mode when it comes to you. Just come over for dinner tonight. We'll brainstorm. I bet between the two of us, we can cook up some genius solution."

I bit my lip. I wanted to tell her how much that pressure

actually weighed on me. How every dollar spent felt like a reminder that we were barely holding it together. But I let it go. Just for now.

Because this—this moment, in our little town, at our favorite café, surrounded by old tables, mismatched chairs, and dusty shelves full of homemade candles and local honey jars, this was the part of life that still felt simple.

And I needed that. Even if just for an hour.

I texted Mom: *Going over to Sarah's for dinner.* She replied almost immediately: *Okay, sounds good.*

I stopped home to change out of my hoodie, swapping it for a flannel shirt, something that looked a little less casual.

By the time I showed up at the Russell's around six, I felt a bit more put together.

I rang the doorbell and waited. Just as I reached to press it again, it opened with a creak.

The face that greeted me made my breath catch. I froze.

Shawn Russell stood at the door, one hand in his pocket, the other holding it open. One earbud dangled; the other was still in. He looked at me with that easy smirk, like he knew exactly what he was doing.

I stuttered. Shawn watched, amused, like he was waiting for me to finish whatever this was.

"Hi," I finally managed, then shuffled into the living room, legs like lead.

"How was practice?" He ruffled my hair as he passed by. I was too flustered to say anything real. Instead, I blurted, "You've got a really nice couch."

"Rion, you've been here a thousand times. That couch's been there forever," Shawn said, glancing over his shoulder.

"And I'm just re-appreciating its beauty," I said, forcing a

26

smile.

He gave me a small grin, shook his head, and disappeared into his room.

Sarah popped up out of nowhere and tugged at my ears. I swiped at hers, but she ducked out of reach and flopped onto the couch. She rested her head in my lap while we half-watched some animated movie on TV.

"Dinner's ready!" Mrs. Russell called from the kitchen.

We took our seats. Mrs. Russell came in with a big bowl of steaming spaghetti and set it in the center of the table. Mr. Russell was already at the head of the table, waiting. She came back with a bowl of meatballs in sauce and placed them next to the pasta.

We dug in. A few minutes passed, and the room stayed quiet except for the clinking of utensils. Shawn's eyes were glued to his phone. Sarah was doing the same.

The silence pressed in on me, thick and uncomfortable. I reached for my phone, tempted to escape into the glow, but I hesitated. The quiet felt suffocating.

"Hand me those phones," Mr. Russell said, his voice firmer than usual.

Shawn looked up, frowning. "What?"

"You've been glued to those screens since we sat down. This is a family dinner, not screen time. Hand them over, I'll give them back after we eat."

They handed over their phones with matching groans, then slumped back into their chairs.

"So, Sarah, Shawn, Rion—how was the first week back?"

Silence. Then Sarah broke it, and we all jumped in—half-talking, half-gesturing like we were trying to outshout each other.

Mrs. Russell smirked. "If that's Gen Z for 'school's fine,' I'll take it."

Shawn muttered something under his breath, which gave Mr. Russell an opening for a dad joke. Somehow, we all ended up laughing.

I stood up fast—too fast. "Uh... bathroom," I said, already halfway out of my chair.

I headed to the bathroom. On my way back, I heard Sarah's voice drift out from the dining room.

"...He only has enough saved for a few more lessons at that tennis club. They raised their prices again. He loves the game so much, and this was supposed to be his next step. I just feel helpless as his best friend."

Oh God, Sarah. Why would you say all that out loud? Now I sound like some kind of charity case.

The table fell silent. Everyone had heard her speech and probably agreed with it.

Mr. Russell cleared his throat. "Rion's a good kid," he said, chewing slowly. "He really loves tennis. I admire how serious he is about it." He looked at his wife. "We could help him out. Right, hon?"

Mrs. Russell nodded. "Sounds like a good idea."

I felt like the air had thickened. My cheeks burned, and my legs itched in my sneakers, but I couldn't hide in the hallway forever.

I took a breath and stepped back in, trying to look normal. Every pair of Russell eyes snapped toward me.

I sat and picked at my food, feeling the silence pressing down like a heavy coat.

"Rion?"

I looked up at Mr. Russell, trying to keep my expression

28

neutral. "Sir?"

"Sarah mentioned you've been having trouble covering the tennis lesson fees and that it's been weighing on you."

I glanced at Sarah. She smiled, gently. The weight of everyone's attention pressed in.

"We want to help you," Mr. Russell said, glancing at his wife. "Michelle and I are good friends with Mr. Rickson, who owns the country club. I'll give him a call after dinner—see if I can pull a few strings and get you a job."

My eyes widened. I caught Shawn grinning at my reaction and quietly chuckling.

Mr. Russell cleared his throat and went on. "This way, you could get a discount on lessons and earn a little money too. We'd also like to pay for the next two months so you can start saving."

My heart soared. I shot up and leaned over to hug Mr. Russell while he was still seated. "Thank you so much, sir."

I turned to Mrs. Russell. "Thank you both. This really means a lot. My mom will be thrilled that we found a solution. Thank you."

Realizing I was still holding on, I let go and sat back down.

Back at the table, I tried to finish eating, but I was buzzing with joy and embarrassment. My mouth twitched into a grin I couldn't control, and I silently begged myself to quit smiling like an idiot.

Chapter 5

I walked home with my head in the clouds.

The late summer air was warm and heavy, wrapping the town in a soft, golden glow. I passed old picket fences and front yards with faded garden gnomes, the kind of small-town charm that made our little place feel frozen in time. Even the cracked sidewalks couldn't ruin my mood. Not today.

Joy bubbled up inside me, light and persistent. Everything felt like it was finally clicking into place, or at least, tennis was. And for me, that was everything. I knew people said lingering on good news was a good way to jinx it, but I didn't care. I kept replaying the day in my head until I was grinning like a lunatic. My cheeks actually ached.

My phone buzzed in my pocket, snapping me out of my reverie. Sarah.

"Hey, Miller," she said, her voice dancing with amusement.

"Why don't you just call me Rion like everyone else?"

I sighed, nudging a loose rock with the tip of my sneaker. The walk was catching up with me, and I was already craving a shower and my bed. I picked up my pace past the little corner gas station that never updated its prices on time.

"Your last name sounds kind of exotic," she teased, slipping into the most sarcastic voice I'd ever heard from her.

I laughed. It echoed a little on the empty road.

"Aye, Captain," she added. "You home yet?"

"Almost."

"Good God. You left our house, like, thirty minutes ago. It only takes fifteen to get home."

"Here comes the math whiz who still couldn't figure out number two," I shot back, mimicking her tone. "It's a solid thirty minutes. Door to door."

"Just... get home safe and try not to get kidnapped. Next time, maybe Shawn drives you."

The idea of being alone in a car with Shawn sent a shock through me—equal parts thrill and terror. My breath caught, and sweat prickled along my upper lip.

I faked a cough. "Byeee, Sarah."

The streets quieted even more as I turned onto my road— gravel shoulders, aging mailboxes, and wide lawns dotted with rusted lawn chairs or leftover Fourth of July decorations no one had taken down. Ours was one of the smaller homes, with flaking siding and wind chimes that hadn't sung in months. But still, it was home.

I reached the front steps and twisted the doorknob.

"Hi, Mom. I'm home," I called.

No answer.

Then—click-clack—Luna's paws on the floor. She bounded into view, tail wagging furiously, nipping at the cuff of my jeans.

"Hey, Lu, you sweet thing." I crouched to stroke her ears and kissed the top of her head. She smelled a little like mud and the Febreze spray mom likes to use on the couch.

I moved toward the hallway and paused outside Mom's room. Her door was slightly ajar.

As usual, she'd fallen asleep at her laptop.

31

She was slumped over the desk she'd had since I was ten, the same one that had followed us through three apartments and now into our little two-bedroom place. The glow from the screen lit up the lines in her face. She looked exhausted.

Mom had worked at a small ad agency in town forever, doing marketing coordination or something equally thankless. She was good at it. Probably better than they deserved. But it never seemed to pay enough, not for how hard she worked.

I hovered in the doorway, debating whether to wake her.

Instead, I carefully slipped the laptop out from beneath her arms, replaced it with a pillow, and eased her head down. She murmured something incoherent but didn't wake. I pulled the fleece throw from the back of her chair and tucked it around her shoulders.

"I love you," I whispered.

Luna circled my legs, brushing against my ankles. I smiled and stretched, the ache in my feet finally catching up with me. Time to ditch the shoes.

I kicked them off into the closet and wandered down the narrow hallway toward the kitchen, where the linoleum tiles were just beginning to peel in one corner. Luna curled up in the living room behind me, her chin resting on one paw like a sleepy guard dog.

Then I remembered the leftovers I'd brought home.

I doubled back to the front door, where my backpack lay in a heap, and unzipped it. I pulled out the tinfoil-wrapped meatballs—Sarah's mom always packed too much—and padded into the kitchen. I dropped one in Luna's bowl.

She looked up at me, wide-eyed.

"Okay," I said. "Just this once."

She inhaled it in one bite. I leaned down, chuckling, and

whispered, "Don't tell Mom. This stays between us."

I glanced at the sink—still full from dinner. The pans, a few mismatched plates, and a half-empty bottle of dish soap.

Might as well help.

I queued up my favorite playlist—mostly retro pop, with a few tracks from Lizzo and Fifth Harmony—and got to work. The warm water and music made it easy. I found my rhythm and scrubbed, rinsed, dried, and stacked.

After, I wiped my hands on a towel and called out, "Come on, girl. Time for bed."

Luna followed me to my room, but flopped right onto a pile of clean laundry before I could stop her. She let out a dramatic sigh. I tried to shift her, and she huffed like I'd just ruined her entire night.

Smirking, I reached for my nightstand and tugged at the bottom drawer. It stuck. It always did. I dug through the mess of junk—old chargers, candy wrappers, crumpled to-do lists— until my fingers brushed something solid.

The picture frame.

I pulled it out slowly. The finish had long since faded. I turned it over, and even in the low light, the image was clear.

Four-year-old me, sitting in a boat with Dad. He held up a sad-looking fish, and we were both grinning like we'd won a trophy. Sunlight sparkled off the water behind us. My arms were tiny. His smile was enormous.

I stared at it, searching for a memory that didn't come.

It felt like a photo from someone else's life. A story I'd heard a hundred times but couldn't actually remember. Still, it meant something. It always would.

I blinked hard, swallowed the tightness in my throat, and placed it back into the drawer.

Luna had shifted to the corner, curling up in the laundry pile like a queen. I stretched out on my bed, one arm folded behind my head, and let the quiet settle in.

Would life have looked different if Dad were still here?

Would we still be in this neighborhood with its flickering streetlamps and pothole-patched roads?

Would Mom sleep more?

Would I have a little brother? A sister?

Would Dad be the one helping me with my tennis swing, tracking my footwork, cheering from the sidelines?

That image—that idea—stuck with me. The two of us, on the court. Laughing. Competing. Him shouting encouragement while I served.

Chapter 6

The hallway by the cafeteria was always the loudest, especially during first and last periods. It was the unofficial hangout spot between the cafeteria and gym, with a straight shot to the student parking lot. Upperclassmen and jocks practically lived there, but Sarah and I only showed up when Shawn gave us a ride, maybe once a week.

Today, for reasons still unclear, we were sitting on the floor before first period.

Sarah and I were glued to our phones, trading dumb celebrity memes. The floor was freezing and needed mopping, but I tried to ignore it. As I scrolled, I caught a few double-takes in our direction. A group passed, and one girl asked, "Is that a new student?" Her friend said, "No, that's some kid named Filler, I think."

I rolled my eyes at the "Filler" bit and turned to Sarah. "Do I have something on my face? Or a weird stain or something?"

She giggled without looking up. "Quite the celebrity now, huh?"

I stared at her, waiting. She sighed—louder this time—then finally looked up with a smirk.

"Miller, look at you! Hair combed, clothes that weren't pulled from the hamper—who are you right now?"

I took a moment to grasp that with my hair clean and combed, and my clothes not looking like they'd been run over by a monster truck, I was suddenly unrecognizable.

I smirked. "You want an autograph?"

"You can sign it on my coffee cup," she said with a grin.

"What are your plans after school today?"

"It's my first day at the club. I'm officially employed. You'd better put some respect on that name."

"Oh yeah?" She laughed. "Try not to mess up on your first day," she said, dragging out her voice as she stood and headed off to class.

Math. First period. I'd survive. I pulled the knob and stepped inside.

Everyone got cold feet. I did too, because I fell under the umbrella of everyone.

I got to the club twenty minutes early and froze the second I reached the front doors. I'd walked through them a hundred times before for lessons, but today felt different. I wasn't a player—I was here for work. Everything looked sharper, more official somehow. The front hedges were perfectly trimmed, the walkway freshly swept, and even the gold-lettered sign seemed more intimidating than usual.

Inside, the familiar scent of fresh-cut grass and lemony floor polish hit me right away. Usually, I headed straight for the courts, but now my eyes darted everywhere—the front desk, the dining area through the glass, the polished wooden beams overhead. There was a buzz of conversation from a few members and the quiet shuffle of staff moving through their routines. For the first time, I wasn't just a kid coming to hit balls. I was sizing the place up like it might be my future.

I counted to ten in my head, willing the nerves to back off. They didn't, but I stepped in anyway.

"Hi," I said to the girl behind the counter. She looked like she could've been in college, older, confident, chewing gum with the ease of someone who'd worked here for years. "Is Mr. Rickson around?"

She looked up from her clipboard. "Oh yeah, he's here. Check the lounge out front—green T-shirt, black pants. You'll spot him easily." She gave me a friendly smile.

"With that kind of fashion statement, I'm sure I will," I joked, trying not to sound like I was completely new at this. "I'm Rion. Rion Miller."

"Sally. Sally Benson." She shook my hand firmly. "Nice to meet you. Are you the new hire?"

I let out a small laugh. "Hopefully. We'll see."

"Well, I hope so. I like your energy already," she said, before disappearing into the back.

I held onto it as I walked past the large windows overlooking the courts. Through the glass, I saw the lounge area: leather chairs, big ceiling fans spinning slowly, the afternoon sun casting long beams across the floor. A few regulars were sipping iced tea or scanning the paper.

There he was, green T-shirt, black pants, just like she said— lounging in one of the chairs with a clipboard on his lap and sunglasses pushed up on his head. I'd been coming here for two summers now, and somehow I'd never actually seen the guy in charge.

"Oh, hey!" he said, springing up like he'd been expecting me. He grabbed my shoulders like he was checking for quality, like

I was a tennis racket he might add to his lineup. "You must be Rion Miller."

"Yes, sir," I said, trying not to flinch under the sudden attention.

"Mr. Russell had great things to say about you," he said, beaming. "We're happy to have you. Sounds like you've got a good head on your shoulders."

He offered his hand. "I'm Mr. Rickson. Or just 'Rickson.' Or 'Sir,' if you're into the whole formality thing." He winked, his tone more laid-back than I expected from someone running a country club.

I smiled. "Thanks. I really appreciate the opportunity."

He led me through the main corridor, past the pro shop and locker rooms, explaining the pay rate, dress code, employee discounts, and a few extra perks, like leftover snacks from catering events, which honestly sounded amazing. The place was familiar and new all at once. I'd never noticed the framed black-and-white photos of championship matches, or the quiet rhythm of how the staff moved, efficient, invisible, part of the club's heartbeat.

We looped back around to the check-in counter, where four other employees were gathered, two guys around my age and two girls. One of them was Sally, who spotted me right away.

"Hey, look who made the cut!" she said brightly.

I gave a small wave. "Yeah. I'm in."

Mr. Rickson gave her a nod. "Sally will show you the ropes, get you trained up. You'll be shadowing this week and doing a little of everything, front desk, locker room clean up, but mostly you'll be in the restaurant."

"Got it," I said, straightening my shoulders a bit.

"Good. Glad to have you on board, Rion." With that, he

headed off to greet a group of members coming in through the side patio, leaving me with the rest of the crew.

Sally turned to me with a knowing smile. "Ready to see what working at a tennis club actually looks like?"

I glanced around, at the clean, sunlit space, the faint echo of serves cracking on the courts outside, the polished image of a world I was about to step into from the other side.

"Yeah," I said. "I think I am."

"All right, let me introduce you to the others and get you a black polo so you fit in a little more.. The guy with glasses is Sev. Long hair is Grace. Short bangs is Chen. Bright eyes is Luke."

They all looked early to mid-twenties, definitely not just out of high school. They waved and smiled, except Sev, whose face stayed neutral. I wondered if Sally was always this bubbly.

"Everyone, meet Rion," she announced with a flourish.

"Rion is one unique name," Sev said. His voice was flat, but not unfriendly.

Everyone laughed, and she led me toward the back.

As we passed through the dining room and into the kitchen, my palms were clammy. My mouth went dry.

Trying to catch up, I mumbled, "So... am I watching training videos back here or something?"

"Training videos?" Sally laughed. "Nope. We're all about the hands-on approach here."

If it were possible, my body tensed even more.

Sally let me know the dinner service would start soon, and the restaurant would begin to pack up.

What felt like moments later, I was balancing a tray of half-eaten lentil soup and carrot-quinoa salad. They smelled amazing. In my left hand, I carried three stacked plates, and in my right, a basket of empty glasses. Grace, helping someone

39

nearby, shot me a worried look.

"You sure you can handle all that?" she asked.

I nodded. But halfway to the counter, the plates tilted and crashed to the floor.

Clang!

Every head turned.

Mortified, I scrambled up, covered in a mess I couldn't even identify. At least nothing broke. Chen came over to help me gather the scratched dishes. We made our way back to the kitchen. When we got through the doors, Chen threw everything in the dish pit and went back to serving like nothing happened.

By 9 PM Friday, I'd officially made it through a full week at the country club. Each day had blurred into the next, but I was mildly proud of sticking it out.

As I waited for the bus, I wondered if this was how Mom felt every week. Being a summer camp counselor for 6-year-olds hadn't prepared me for real work.

I had dropped drinks, folded towels and tablecloths wrong, and delivered orders to the wrong tables. By the end of the week, I'd broken four dishes and six glasses, and once served meat to a vegetarian. I thought it was tofu or one of those fake meat things. It wasn't.

I felt like a worn-out kangaroo that had hopped across Australia, and I spent the entire ride home with my head in my lap.

Later, lying in bed, I called Sarah.

"Sarah, I can't do this. You don't get it—it's only been a week, and everything's already falling apart," I said, pressing the phone hard against my ear.

"Miller, breathe—"

So I did. I exhaled. Inhaled. Exhaled again.

40

Slowly, my thoughts untangled.

"There, that's it. Remember why you took this job—tennis. This is just the start. You're adjusting. You'll figure it out," Sarah said.

"I don't know, Sarah. I really don't know," I said, my voice unsteady.

The first few weeks of juggling my job, school, and tennis training hadn't been easy. I tried to console myself with the phrase, "Good things don't come easy." It gave me something to hold onto—proof I could keep going. But when my back ached from hauling food and drinks for club members, and I could barely bend down to tie my shoes in the school bathroom, I started to realize I might've taken on too much.

By the end of the day, I shuffled down the hallway like a zombie. Every step felt like a chore, and my brain was sludge.

"Gotcha."

An arm yanked me into a headlock out of nowhere, elbows crushing my ears. I tapped at her arm, trying to signal a surrender.

"I'm tapping."

"This isn't wrestling, Miller," Sarah laughed. She was way too pleased with herself, which just made it worse.

I finally pried her arm off and ran a hand through my hair, now sticking out in every direction.

"You really need to stop that," I glared at her.

She stepped back, hands on her hips, giving me a teasing once-over.

"Oh, who's gonna stop me?"

I rolled my eyes, stuck out my tongue, and sighed.

Sarah pulled me into a hug, resting my head on her shoulder.

"Ugh, what are you doing, Sarah?"

"Poor Rion. So stressed lately, huh? You need a massage and a trip to Hawaii," she said lightly.

She linked our arms as we walked down the hall. I heard her mutter something under her breath.

"Mianhae."

"What's that?" I asked, caught off guard.

"That's Korean for sorry."

I stopped and turned to her. "When did you learn Korean?"

She launched into a rant about some Korean show, something with K-pop stars and YouTube. I zoned out as we kept walking.

Outside, I cut into her rant about K-pop stars. "Let's go to the Honey Hive."

"Okay." She let go of my arm, then yelped, "Oh, wait! Shoot! Mom needs me this afternoon. I can't make it."

From behind us we heard, "Oh, going alone? Need a date, Filler Miller?"

I spun around, glaring. "Are you obsessed with me or something?"

Jason's only response was to fake gag like he was about to throw up. I rolled my eyes and walked toward the Honey Hive.

I sipped my iced honey vanilla latte, trying to calm down. Jason always left me rattled, and I hated that he could get under my skin like that.

I was still stewing when the door opened. I looked up just in time to see Shawn head to the counter. My heart jumped, and I suddenly had no idea what to do with my hands. I scribbled random nonsense in my notebook.

Two taps on the table snapped me out of it. I looked up and

sucked in a sharp breath. Shawn was standing there, amused. He reached out, ruffled my hair, and pulled out the chair next to me.

He didn't say anything at first, just leaned back in the chair like he'd been planning to sit there all along. His backpack hit the floor with a soft thud.

"So," he said after a moment. "Rough day?"

I scoffed in his general direction, but not at him directly. "You looked like you were about to stab your notebook."

I glanced down at the chaotic scribbles on the page. "I was venting."

"Looks like a murder confession."

I chuckled in spite of myself, then sighed and leaned back in my chair. "Just tired. Work's been... a lot. And school on top of it. And Jason being Jason."

He nudged my foot under the table. "Seriously, though. I get why you're tired. But you're doing it, Rion. Like, actually doing it. Tennis. Work. School. Life."

I looked at him. "Barely."

"Still counts."

We sat in silence for a few beats, the noise of the café fading into the background. I could feel the weight in my chest start to shift. Shawn pulled out notebooks, and I went back to attempting to study.

Chapter 7

Another day, another class. Oddly enough, the gym teacher, Mr. Konnor, also coached half the school's sports teams. He made everyone call him "Coach"— whether they played for him or not.

As the class sat on the uncomfortable gym floor, I thought, *Has this floor ever been cleaned? How does the basketball team even play here?*

Mr. Konnor stood stiffly at the front, hands jammed in his pockets like he was about to deliver classified intel.

"We're starting a new unit today, and I bet some of you are wondering what it is—"

Jason cut in. "Oh wow, tennis nets and rackets. Who could've guessed? Really subtle setup. Ten out of ten for suspense."

A few snickers floated across the gym. I rolled my eyes. *When will he stop being such a jerk?*

Mr. Konnor, clearly annoyed but holding it together, cleared his throat. "As Jason so helpfully pointed out, we're starting racket sports—starting with tennis. Today is about proper grip and basic volleys. This is coordination training, so I expect full effort."

He divided the class into four groups. With only two nets, it was simple—one group per side. Everyone started sizing each other up.

Naturally, because the universe had a sense of humor, I found myself facing Jason across the net. Of course.

But then something clicked. *Maybe this isn't a total disaster. No—this is perfect. I finally get to shut him up on a court. My court.*

Mr. Konnor blew his whistle like he was starting a horse race.

I headed for the pile of beat-up rackets, thinking I'd seen rackets in better shape at a garage sale. Choosing a weathered but solid racket, I took my place on the court.

A ball was struck with an excessive amount of force from Jason's side of the net.

I split-stepped, racket angled in a textbook grip. Time slowed as he met the ball with a clean volley, sending it skimming low over the net. The ball flew past Jason, bounced twice, and was gone before he could even react.

"Point. Fifteen-love," I called, steady and loud.

The silence that followed tasted sweet.

Jason's stunned expression curdled into a scowl. Eyes narrowed, jaw clenched—I knew trouble was coming. Jason's face flushed a deep red. He wasn't just embarrassed—he was humiliated. And that meant he'd retaliate.

"Every loser has their day," Jason snapped, raising his voice like he had an audience. Pulling a ball from his pocket, he slammed the ball high into the air.

"Good luck getting that one, Miller!"

I didn't even pause. I pivoted and sprinted toward the back of the court, tracking the ball with laser focus. My body kicked into gear—feet pounding, eyes locked, every movement automatic. I didn't even notice the other students scrambling to get out of his way.

The shot was overcooked—too much force. I had already read

45

it. The ball started to drop just past the baseline.

Still in stride, I twisted mid-run, facing away from the court. The ball bounced once—I was ready. I widened my stance, hopped slightly, and snapped my racket between his legs.

My first-ever tweener sailed over the net, floating past Jason with the confidence of someone who'd done it a hundred times.

The gym went dead silent, except for the whoosh of the ball. Highlight-reel stuff. And Jason? Just standing there. Again.

Mr. Konnor's whistle cut through the silence, signaling rotation. A double whistle followed—gym class was over. The students scattered toward the locker rooms.

I walked off, still buzzing from the shot, ready to shake off the adrenaline.

Then I heard it.

"Rion."

I froze mid-step, palms suddenly clammy. Mr. Konnor was looking straight at me and heading over. My heart rate kicked up.

What did I do?

I flexed my fingers, trying to shake off the nerves.

"Hey, Rion," Mr. Konnor said. His voice is calm. "Nice play out there. Have you played tennis before?"

"I, uh... I play a lot. I train at a country club," I said, my voice wavering. "I—I work there too."

Why did I say that?

Mr. Konnor nodded, a small smile forming. "You've got real skill," he said, eyeing me like he was sizing me up. "You should try out for varsity in the spring."

I blinked, then laughed nervously. "I'd love to. Th-thank you, Coach."

"Call me Coach Konnor," he said, smirking slightly as he

46

walked away.

I stood still for a moment, my heart pounding.

Varsity tennis.

As I headed to the locker room, still dazed from the conversation, I ran straight into Jason.

Of course.

Jason's smug grin bloomed the moment he saw me.

"Well, if it isn't our tennis star, Rion Miller. Let's give it up, folks!"

Jason clapped, slow and loud, the sound bouncing off the walls as he circled me like a predator. I turned away and focused on his locker, pulling off my gym shirt and changing fast.

"What—so now you think you're better than everyone else just because you can swing a racket?"

Jason leaned in close. The smell of cheap cologne hit my nose.

"I never said that, Jason," I muttered, pulling on a clean shirt.

But Jason wasn't done. He snatched the jeans I had pulled from my locker and set them on the bench—then, grinning, walked toward the back exit.

"You want these?" he said, holding them up like they were trash. "Come and get 'em."

I lunged, but Jason darted out the door.

I stood frozen in my boxers, face flushed with heat and shame.

Outside the gym, Jason sauntered to the dumpster, dropped the jeans in, and turned back with a sickly sweet smile.

My blood boiled as I stomped back to my locker, yanking my gym shorts back on in a mad scramble, nearly face-planting in the process. I cursed under my breath, anger surging through my body, when suddenly, my phone buzzed from inside my locker. Frowning, I grabbed it, half-expecting a text from Sarah. But it was from mom.

I opened the message, and my heart sank.

"RION. WHEN I GET HOME TONIGHT WE NEED TO HAVE A TALK ABOUT YOUR SCIENCE TEST!"

My eyes widened. All caps. That was never a good sign. How did she find out so quickly? And then it hit me.

Of course—Mr. Saltzman, my science teacher, who I'm sure had it out for me, said he was going to contact all parents whenever someone failed a test.

I slammed my fist into the locker door, the loud metallic clang echoing through the room as frustration and embarrassment collided inside of me.

"Mr. Saltzman, you snitch," I groaned as I walked to the dumpster. It felt like the universe had just handed me a double gut punch.

Chapter 8

Lately, I'd been putting in double the effort with my studies, still shaken from the disaster that was last week's science test. I'd barely studied, too wiped out after back-to-back work shifts and tennis lessons at the club, and it showed. I bombed it so badly that I thought my mom was going to ground me for life. So, I made a quiet promise to myself. Do better, keep it together.

At the moment, I was in my usual spot at the Honey Hive, tucked into the back corner. I'd been glued to my books for three hours straight. My eyes were heavy, my brain buzzing with fatigue, and the words on the page had started to blur. I took a break and scrolled through Instagram—just enough to reset before diving back in.

I lifted my head from the stack of textbooks, stretched my neck, and glanced around the room. The Honey Hive was nearly empty, except for someone rustling behind the counter. Squinting through the dim light and the fog of exhaustion, I tried to make out who it was.

Then his head popped up. Shawn.

Of course.

I immediately blushed. I'd forgotten he was working tonight. His apron was slightly crooked, like he'd thrown it on mid-rush, and he was fumbling behind the counter—probably fixing the coffee machine or restocking supplies.

He caught my eye and grinned, a little lopsided. "Still here, huh?"

I smiled back awkwardly, barely peeking over my books. He nodded and went back to what he was doing, and I forced myself to focus again—for at least ten more minutes.

Before I knew it, the sky had gone dark. I mentally kicked myself. How had time slipped away again? I scrambled to pack up, fumbling with my zipper and muttering under my breath. Just as I was about to rush out, Shawn popped up, wiping his hands on a rag.

"Rion," he called out, voice warm, teasing.

"Hey, Shawn," I said, stuffing the last book into my bag. "Sorry I stayed so late. I got lost in studying."

He crossed his arms, smirking. "So it's safe to call you a nerd now? Sarah's not with you?"

I laughed, slinging my bag over my shoulder. "Me? A nerd? Nah. I'm just trying not to fail again. And Sarah's probably at the library torturing herself with flashcards."

He waved me off, smile softening. "It's fine. I'm closing up in ten. You can hang out. I'll lock up and drop you off at home."

He raised his right hand in mock solemnity, placing his left over his heart like he was swearing an oath. I chuckled and set my bag back down. His gaze lingered a second longer than usual, and my heart fluttered.

With a quick ruffle of my hair, he disappeared behind the counter.

I looked down at the floor, smiling to myself as I sank into the chair. Exhaustion finally hit.

Ten minutes later, Shawn plopped down beside me with a sigh and closed his eyes. I glanced sideways, pulse quickening.

He looked wiped out. I wanted to say something, offer some kind of comfort—but the words jammed in my throat.

Then he broke the silence.

"Here you go," he said, sliding a small box across the table.

"What's this?" I asked, shaking the box lightly.

Shawn gasped, covering his mouth. "Rion! You just broke the number one mystery box rule!"

I froze. "What rule?"

"Never shake a mystery box," he said, like it was obvious. "Could be breakables. Could be bugs. Don't risk it."

I rolled my eyes. "Aye, captain." I gave him a mock salute and opened the box. Inside were snacks. Homemade, by the look of them.

"Are you sure this won't get docked from your paycheck?" I asked.

He laughed. "Nah. Leftovers. No harm, no foul."

I pulled out a scone, took a bite, and nodded. "Did you make these?"

He rubbed the back of his neck. "Yeah, with a few of the other workers. I like baking. It's kind of my side hustle. I'm thinking maybe culinary school, eventually."

"That's amazing," I said. "You should go for it."

He nudged my shoulder. "Thanks. But what about you? What's your big plan?"

I hesitated. "It's not huge, but... I want to be a pro tennis player one day."

Shawn raised his eyebrows. "Not huge? That's massive."

I groaned, giving him a light push. "Don't do that."

"Do what?" he said, grinning.

"You know what."

We stared at each other, half-glaring, half-smiling, until he

51

burst out laughing.

"You've gotta see your face when you try to act tough," he said between laughs.

I shook my head. "You're impossible."

Still smiling, I raised my scone. He raised a donut.

"Cheers to tennis and to pastry school," I said.

We clinked our pastries together.

Chapter 9

Shawn dropped me off at home, just like he promised. The ride was a blur of laughter, bad jokes, and shouting lyrics at the top of our lungs. For a moment, the world felt easy. As I climbed out of the car and waved, Shawn gave me a wink. I thought I imagined it, until he smirked and pulled away. That wink stayed with me longer than I wanted to admit.

I shook my head. Get it together.

The door was locked, no surprise. Mom was working late again. I grabbed the spare key from under the rock. I was too lazy to look for my house keys floating somewhere in my bag. I stepped into the empty house and was hit by silence. Heavy, familiar, annoying.

I nearly stepped on Luna, curled up by the shoe rack. She groaned as I scooped her up, not even trying to hide her displeasure.

I collapsed onto the couch with her beside me. The quiet pressed in.

No Dad. No Mom. Just me and this stupid quiet.

I pulled out my phone. Scrolled. Almost texted Sarah. Then my phone buzzed. Her name lit up the screen.

"You know," I said as I picked up, "I was just about to call you—"

"We're totally in sync," she interrupted. I could hear her grin. "My brother said he dropped you off. Everything okay?"

I thought about the wink. The drive. That warm feeling.

"Yeah, I'm good," I said. "Got carried away at the Honey Hive. He offered to drop me."

"Cool. Meet me at the gas station in ten? I need a slushie. Also, I've got something to tell you."

Something in her voice made me pause. Curious, a little nervous.

"Sure," I said. "Be there soon."

I gave Luna a quick pat, then stepped back into the fading light. The sky was soft purple, the air cooling off as the sun slid behind the hills. Five minutes later, I found Sarah at the slushie machine, cup half-full with radioactive blue syrup.

"Took you long enough," she teased as I joined her at the counter.

"Yeah, yeah." I filled my cup, and we paid.

Outside, we leaned against the brick wall, drinks in hand, the warm night air humming with the buzz of a neon sign overhead. For a moment, we just sipped in silence. The kind of pause that feels loaded before you even realize why.

"So," I said finally, trying to keep it casual, "how's tutoring?"

That one word, tutoring, was like flipping a switch. Her shoulders tensed. She took a long sip without looking at me, eyes suddenly trained on something far away.

"Yeah, about that..." she said, voice tight.

"What?" I asked, trying to read her expression. "Did something happen?"

She kept fidgeting with her straw, twisting the paper wrapper around it like it might offer a distraction or an answer.

"You know how I've been tutoring Jason a lot lately?"

54

My stomach sank. "Yeah..."

She glanced up at me, just for a second. "We're dating."

The words didn't register at first. They just hovered in the air between us. Then they slammed down like bricks.

"Jason? Jason Banks?" My voice cracked with disbelief.

She nodded, biting her lip like she already knew how I'd react. "I know how it sounds, but he's really not as bad as you think."

I stared at her, stunned. "He's a bully, Sarah. You've seen it. He's bullied me."

She crossed her arms. "I know, but... he's different around me. Plus, he's the first real guy to show any interest in me. I think he acts out to fit in. He doesn't mean it."

I looked away, swallowing hard. The first dozen responses in my head were sharp, but none made it past my lips. I felt them there, tight in my chest, caught in my throat, but I said nothing. Not yet.

I let out a short breath that sounded like a laugh but wasn't. "So what, I should just forget everything? Just because he's nice to you?"

She looked hurt. "I didn't want to lie. I just... I wanted you to hear it from me."

Silence stretched between us. I stared out at the parking lot, forcing my face to stay neutral.

She stepped closer. "Please. I just want you to be happy for me. I'll talk to him. I'll ask him to stop."

I nodded once, carefully. "I'll try," I said. It was the only truth I could give her in that moment. I wasn't ready to forgive her. Not fully. Not yet. But I also didn't want to lose her.

She stepped forward and hugged me. I didn't move at first. My arms stayed limp at my sides. Part of me wanted to lean into it, let it mean something. Another part wanted to pull away and ask her what the hell she was thinking. Dating Jason?

"Thanks, maybe the nerd can end up with a jock" she whispered.

I didn't answer. My thoughts were too tangled. A loop of Jason Banks? Seriously? Kept playing on repeat in my head. This wasn't some random guy. This was the person who made my life miserable. Who humiliated me. Who seemed to take joy in it. And she knew that.

And now she wanted to change the subject.

"So, you?" she said, with forced cheer. "Any crushes?"

I blinked at her. "You've got to be kidding."

"Come on. Girl in our class?"

I shook my head. "No, Sarah. Not a girl."

She paused for a second, then her eyes lit up. "Boy, then?"

I froze. The words jammed in my throat. My heart thudded like I'd just been asked to walk out on stage with no clothes on.

"Uh..."

But she just smiled gently, like she was handing me a life preserver. "It's okay, Rion. I already know."

"You... know?"

She raised an eyebrow. "Yeah. And you didn't tell me?" She gave me a playful shove. "Some best friend you are."

"I wasn't ready," I said, barely above a whisper.

She pulled me into a hug again, tighter this time. "I get it. I'm just glad you're you."

I laughed, but it came out as more of a breath. "Are you trying to crush me or comfort me?"

She grinned. "Both."

We stood there in silence, sipping our blue slushies as the sky melted into pinks and oranges. Crickets started up, and the neon sign above us hummed like a lullaby.

I didn't say the words. Not really. But she knew.
And she was still here.
Still Sarah.

Chapter 10

I heard the sounds. They were definitely words, forming sentences, spilling from my teacher's mouth as she paced at the front of the classroom. Sweat glistened on her face. Her hands moved in sharp, animated bursts. Her eyes scanned the room for signs of life.

But fatigue was winning. My eyelids sagged, the edges of the room softened, and her voice faded to a low hum. I was losing the fight.

Then—suddenly—a jolt.

"RION!"

My name punched through the fog. A tap on my shoulder followed, more like a shove. I snapped upright with a gasp, blinking hard as the classroom slammed into focus.

My heart thudded. Every eye was on me.

From the back:

"Welcome back, Sleeping Beauty."

Laughter exploded around me—sharp, cutting, merciless. My face flushed hot. I clenched my fists under the desk, wishing the floor would open up and swallow me whole.

My teacher, Mrs. Johnson, marched toward me. Her expression was drenched in disappointment.

"Didn't sleep enough last night, Rion Miller?" Her tone was

sharp but not loud.

"I... I did, ma'am," I mumbled.

"So what's going on?" she asked, crossing her arms. "Why are you falling asleep in my class?"

The room went quiet again. Even the air seemed to freeze.

"I... I don't know," I mumbled, eyes on the desk, shrinking smaller with each word.

She tilted her head. "Do you think this is a good use of your time?"

"No... It's not th-that." My voice wavered. I felt like a trapped animal under her gaze.

She took a breath and softened, just barely. "See me in my office after school."

With that, she turned on her heel and continued the lesson like nothing had happened.

The rest of the day passed in a blur. I couldn't focus. Just one long countdown to the conversation I couldn't escape. When the final bell rang, I dragged myself down the hallway, weaving through students eager to get out. I passed two juniors talking about an upcoming calculus quiz, a girl with a sketchbook tucked under her arm, and someone laughing too loudly. Life kept moving.

My teacher's office door was ajar. I hesitated, then stepped inside.

The room was cool and well-lit. She looked up from her desk, calm but serious, and motioned for me to sit. I did, my hands twitching in my lap.

"Rion," she said, voice lower now, "I didn't call you in just because you dozed off today. Your last few assignments have been late. Your quiz scores in biology and algebra have slipped. And I haven't seen your writing journal since the start of the quarter."

I stared at a spot on the floor. "I've been tired. I've been... training. And I work part-time now too."

She leaned forward slightly, tapping her fingers together. "Tennis, right?"

I nodded.

"I'm not here to make your life harder," she said. "But something's got to give. You're capable of more than what I'm seeing. If your performance doesn't improve within a week, I'll have to contact your mother."

I looked up, alarmed. "Please don't. I'll catch up. I promise. Just—please don't tell her."

She held my gaze for a long moment. "One week. Show me some effort. Turn in your missing work. Ask for help if you need it."

I nodded quickly. "Yes. Thank you."

"Alright. "You're dismissed."

As I left her office, my shoulders were tight, but at least I had a deadline. And maybe a chance.

*　*　*

Later that week, I met Sarah in the school library. We had our usual spot tucked between the English section and a dusty globe no one ever touched. The hush of the library wrapped around us like a familiar blanket, but today it didn't feel as comforting.

My backpack exploded across the table—biology textbook, algebra workbook, and a thick packet of English assignments I'd missed. The pressure to catch up was crushing, but my brain refused to cooperate. Every time I tried to focus, my thoughts drifted—to Sarah, to Jason, to the two of them together. I hated that it was getting in the way.

"You're zoning out again," she said, nudging me with her elbow.

"Yeah, sorry." I rubbed my eyes. "It's just... a lot."

She nudged me again, gentler this time. "We'll figure it out. You've got a ton going on, but you're not alone. What's been the hardest?"

"Honestly? Biology labs and algebra quizzes. And Mrs. Johnson is probably one late assignment away from calling my mom."

Sarah opened her notebook, already flipping to a page of neat, color-coded notes. "Let's start with the quiz review. I made flashcards."

"How are you like this?" I asked, managing a smile despite myself.

"Because you need me," she replied with a wink.

We worked for over an hour. She explained osmosis with the energy of someone hosting a science show and made me redo a polynomial equation until I didn't mess it up. Her calm made it easier to keep trying—even if part of me still felt weird, sitting here pretending everything was like before.

I tried not to think about Jason. I tried not to picture her getting those same smiles and study help from him. But the thought hovered just behind every word she said.

Eventually, she leaned back and stretched. "Okay. Brain break."

"Gladly," I said, sinking into my chair.

She grinned. "Thanksgiving's coming. What are you and your mom doing?"

I blinked. "Probably nothing. She'll be working."

"You should come to our place," she said. "You know my

mom will ask about you anyway. Might as well show up for food."

I hesitated. The idea of sitting around her family's table while he might be there... it made my stomach twist. But I missed them. I missed her. I missed the ease we used to have.

"I'll ask her," I said.

"You better," she replied, already smiling like it was a done deal.

I wasn't sure how I felt about it. But at least for now, I wanted to believe her.

Chapter 11

The past few weeks had flown by, a blur of tennis practice, schoolwork, and shifts at the country club. Somewhere in the middle of it all, something shifted. Maybe it was the reset after Thanksgiving. Maybe I'd finally found my rhythm. But my game was improving, and for once, I felt in control.

That afternoon's lesson with Coach Moore confirmed it. The air was crisp—winter creeping in, but perfect for drills inside the tennis bubble.

I gripped my racket, eyes on the baseline, waiting for the next ball. It came fast, but I moved quickly, sliding into position and ripping a clean backhand across the net. The satisfying thwack of the ball on strings told me I'd hit it right.

Coach Moore, pacing along the sideline, let out a low whistle. "Now that's what I'm talking about, Rion. Your backhand's got some Agassi to it today."

I wasn't sure if he meant it or if he was messing with me— his dry humor always kept me guessing, but I smiled anyway. Coming from him, it felt like a win.

All those months of footwork, repetition, and drills were finally syncing. I wasn't just powering through balls anymore. I was placing them—sharp, clean, and deliberate.

"You're playing with intention," he said, nodding. "That's

what separates decent players from great ones."

"Thanks, Coach," I said, bouncing on my feet, the adrenaline still buzzing. "I've been trying to stay consistent."

"It's paying off." He motioned for another round, and I fired off a tight volley that skimmed just above the net. "But keep your focus. Precision, always."

I nodded, already scanning for the next shot. There was still a long way to go, but I wasn't where I started. And that mattered.

After practice, I headed into the club restaurant for my shift.

I'd been working there for a few months as a busser. It had been overwhelming at first—balancing trays, dodging servers, keeping up with the chaos, but I'd adjusted. The rhythm didn't scare me anymore.

The dining room buzzed with end-of-day energy: couples sipping wine, golfers swapping stories, waitstaff weaving through tables. It all felt familiar now.

In the kitchen, Sally and Sev, which I recently learned was short for Seven, were already prepping. They'd both been here longer than me, and never missed a chance to tease.

"Remember your first day?" Sev asked with a grin, wiping down a counter. "You looked like a ghost when that tray crashed."

Sally laughed, stacking napkins into perfect towers. "So pale, Rion. I thought you were gonna bolt."

I shook my head, loading plates onto a tray. "I didn't know restaurants could go from zero to chaos in ten seconds."

"Well, you're a pro now," Sally said, nudging me.

"Yeah, just don't drop anything else," Sev added.

"That was you last week," I said, handing him the tray.

We laughed. The shift passed quickly clearing tables, pouring water, sneaking bites of leftover bread in the back hallway. I was confident now. Capable. I belonged.

Later that week, I met Coach Moore again for a private lesson. My footwork was cleaner. My swings were more efficient. I moved with control.

As I packed up to leave, Coach Moore called out. "Rion."

I turned, a little winded. "Yeah?"

He stepped toward the net, resting one hand on the tape. "You're doing great. But there's something I want to bring up, something that might take your game even further."

I waited, curious.

"Your racket," he said, nodding toward it. "It's outdated. Decent enough, but it's holding you back. Have you ever considered switching to a pro-grade model?"

I looked down at it. The grip was worn, the paint chipped. I'd used it for years.

"I've thought about it," I admitted. "But is it really that different?"

He gave a half-shrug, half-smirk. "Night and day. Lighter, better balance, more control. And easier on your joints. Your shoulder will thank you."

I flexed my arm, thinking about the soreness that crept in after long practices.

"But they're expensive," I said quietly.

Coach Moore nodded. "They are. But you don't have to commit. The pro shop lets you demo a few. Try one before you decide."

That made sense. Try before I buy. No harm in testing.

"Alright," I said. "I'll look into it."

Coach Moore clapped me on the shoulder. "Don't let your gear hold you back. You've got the talent."

As I walked off the court, his words replayed in my mind.

Maybe it was time. If the equipment could take me further, it was worth considering.

I passed the pro shop on my way out, eyes drifting toward the display rack by the window. I made a mental note to ask about demos.

One step at a time.

That night, during my shift in the restaurant, I moved through the dining room with a rhythm that felt natural, balancing trays without second-guessing, trading quick jokes with Sally, nodding at familiar guests like I belonged there. I wasn't just getting through the job anymore. I was finding my stride.

At one point, I caught my reflection in the window, shirt a little untucked, hair slightly out of place, but standing taller than I remembered. Steady. Sure of myself. For once, my mind wasn't looping on Shawn.

I was focused on tomorrow. On tennis. On everything this might lead to.

Chapter 12

The fluorescent lights in the library buzzed faintly overhead, casting a sterile glow across the rows of desks and overstuffed shelves. The air was still, too still. Pages turned somewhere behind me, and the occasional whisper broke the silence, but otherwise, the world had gone quiet.

Too quiet for the storm inside my head.

I hunched over my textbook, eyes locked on the equations in front of me. If I failed another test, I risked more than detention or a parent email—there'd be no spring tennis tryouts, no more private lessons. I couldn't afford to mess up again. Not with everything I was balancing.

But no matter how hard I tried, the numbers blurred on the page. My focus slipped.

My fingers twitched. My mind drifted again to the court. I could almost feel the grip of my racket, the smooth pull of a backhand. Under the table, my arm moved through the motion automatically, muscle memory taking over.

"Rion?"

Sarah's voice cut through the haze.

She dropped into the seat across from me, letting her bag hit the floor with a satisfying thud. Her hair was pulled into a high, messy ponytail, and she wore the look of someone who'd conquered a dozen battles already today. Determined. Fierce. Just enough chaos in her eyes to make it clear she was on a mission.

She raised an eyebrow. "Practicing volleys during study hall?"

I pulled my hand off my invisible racket and flushed. "Didn't even realize I was doing it."

Sarah grinned as she pulled out her notebook, flipping directly to the correct page. "That's why I'm here. To save your distracted tennis brain from flunking algebra."

"Thanks for meeting me, I'm seriously drowning."

She winked. "Let's talk payment. I accept slushies, snacks, or eternal gratitude."

Despite myself, I smiled. Just like that, the air felt lighter. She always knew how to snap me out of it.

We dove into the session. Sarah broke down each formula like she was narrating a crime scene—confident, precise, even a little dramatic. Her pencil moved like it had a mind of its own, sketching examples, drawing graphs, and circling terms I kept forgetting.

Still, my concentration faltered. I caught myself mid-swing under the table again.

Sarah paused, one eyebrow raised. "Rion. Seriously?"

"Sorry," I said quickly, tucking my hands into my lap.

She burst into laughter—just loud enough to earn a sharp glare from the librarian. Sarah clamped her hand over her mouth, eyes dancing.

"You're unreal," she whispered. "Tennis is basically your religion."

I shrugged. "It's kind of hard-wired at this point."

"Well, if you want to pass this test, maybe try praying to the

68

math gods instead."

I chuckled. Sarah's teasing worked like a reset button. I focused. Slowly, the problems stopped looking like alien code and started to click into place.

♦ ♦ ♦

A few days later, after gym class, I lingered in the locker room longer than usual. Most of the guys had already cleared out, their voices echoing down the hallway. I moved slowly, towel around my neck, mind still fuzzy from drills.

Just as I reached the door, voices on the other side of the door stopped me.

Jason. And Sarah.

I froze, my hand on the handle.

"You've been glued to him lately," Jason snapped. His voice was sharp, carrying that same cocky indifference he always wore like armor. "You tutoring everyone now, or just your little friend?"

I held my breath.

Sarah's reply was firm. "He's my best friend, Jason. He asked for help. That's it."

Jason scoffed. "Don't pretend like that's all it is. It's pathetic. He follows you around like a lost puppy."

The word hit like a slap. Pathetic.

My throat tightened.

"Shut up, Jason," Sarah snapped. "You don't get to talk about Rion like that."

There was no hesitation. No doubt. She wasn't backing down.

"I helped you when you were bombing English," she added. "What makes this any different?"

69

A beat of silence. Then Jason muttered something under his breath. Dismissive, distant. Their footsteps moved away.

I stood there, frozen in place. Sarah had stood up for me. Again. But instead of feeling grateful, my stomach twisted. She said Jason was different when they were alone, but here he was, still the same loudmouthed jerk in front of everyone else. Something about that didn't sit right. I wanted to feel relieved, validated even, but all I felt was the sting of being reminded that I still needed defending. And that maybe Jason hadn't changed at all.

Later that week, in math class, snow began to fall outside the window, light flakes drifting down in a slow, lazy dance. The sky had gone soft and gray, and everything felt muffled.

"Rion?"

I turned to see my teacher, Mrs. Johnson, standing beside my desk, holding out a paper.

A red B+ circled at the top.

"I can tell you've been working hard," she said, her voice softer than usual. "Keep this up."

"Thank you," I whispered.

My heart swelled.

It wasn't an A. It wasn't perfect. But it was progress. It was proof that all the effort—the late nights, the tutoring, the moments of doubt—hadn't been wasted.

As I walked out of class and into the snowy afternoon, I felt the cold air hit my face. I smiled. My grades were improving. My tennis game was stronger. And more than anything else, I wasn't alone.

Sarah had my back.

And for the first time in a long time, I believed I was going to be okay.

Chapter 13

The weather kept shifting, like it couldn't decide between autumn and winter. The air had turned colder. Every few days, it snowed—light at first, a dusting that melted by noon. But each time, it lingered longer only to vanish again by morning.

Between school, tennis, and my job at the country club, I could barely breathe. My tennis game was improving, and somehow, my grades hadn't tanked. But every day felt like a sprint through quicksand, one wrong slip and I'd be under.

The Honey Hive had become my escape. A quiet pocket of calm in the middle of the chaos. Even in the freezing cold, I stuck to my usual, an iced honey vanilla latte. Shawn had started giving them to me for free, probably because Sarah was with Jason and he felt bad. But it wasn't just the drink. It was the ritual, something steady when everything else felt like a storm I couldn't outrun.

I sat in my usual window spot, pretending to do homework. My books were open, but I wasn't seeing the pages. Outside, the world looked still, leaves scraping across the sidewalk, faint gold sunlight stretching through bare branches, people wrapped in scarves and coats. It all felt distant, like a life I wasn't part of.

A soft tap on my table pulled me back.

"Daydreaming again?"

Shawn's voice cut through the haze. I looked up to see him standing beside me with a rag in hand, mid-clean. His eyes were narrowed slightly, but a familiar smile tugged at his lips.

I sat up straighter, trying to play it cool. "Yeah, sorry. Just... thinking too much."

He leaned against the back of the chair across from me, smirk deepening. "You've been here, what—an hour? Still staring at the same blank page."

I glanced at my untouched notebook and let out a low sigh. "I just needed a break."

He tapped the table with the rag, mock-serious. "Sure that break doesn't involve zoning out half the time?"

I lifted my cup in a mock toast. "This drink's the real reason I come here. I gave up pretending ages ago."

Shawn chuckled. "Just don't let the view outside keep you from the work inside."

Before I could reply, the door swung open with a jingle. I froze mid-motion, hand still on my pen.

Jason walked in. Ashley was right behind him.

Of all people—why them?

I hadn't seen Jason much lately. Maybe because Sarah had told him to back off. But that didn't mean I trusted him. And Ashley? She was always close to Jason, too close. The way they exchanged glances, laughed at things no one else understood. It was more than friendship. I'd bet on it.

My pulse quickened. A dull buzz of irritation rose in my ears. This was supposed to be my safe space. I didn't need their chaos invading it.

Shawn stepped off to the side, his expression unreadable.

I started to stand, but Jason's hand clamped onto the back of

73

my chair, holding me down.

"Whoa—where are you going, Rion? We're just chatting. No need to bolt."

The café quieted, like it sensed something was about to shift.

Jason leaned in, voice low and poisonous. "Or are you running off because Sarah already told me your little secret? Scared someone else might figure it out?"

The floor dropped out from under me.

No. He didn't mean that. Sarah wouldn't tell him. She couldn't.

Would she?

I'd trusted her. But the thought cracked something inside me.

Jason leaned back, eyes glinting.

"What? You didn't know, Ash?" he said louder, loud enough to pierce the room. "Rion's into guys. Think he's hoping Shawn finally notices."

Silence fell.

Conversations died. The warmth drained from the café. I could feel the eyes—every single one.

They were all staring.

I couldn't breathe. My lungs clenched. My heart thundered. My hands trembled as the heat in my face turned to ice.

Jason's words echoed, louder with each repeat.

I stood too fast, almost knocking over my chair. "I—I have to go," I muttered, barely audible.

Across the table, Shawn stiffened. His brows pulled together, eyes darting from Jason to me.

My hands shook so violently I could barely zip my bag. I blinked hard, a tear slipping down before I could stop it. I wiped it away fast, but it didn't matter. Everyone had already seen.

I shoved past Jason and bolted.

The cold air outside hit me like a slap, but it didn't help. My legs carried me down the sidewalk on autopilot, past storefronts and bus stops, away from everyone and everything.

Jason's voice chased me like a shadow I couldn't outrun. At the far end of the street, I finally dropped onto a bench and buried my face in my hands.

The tears came fast. Hot. Ugly.

I tried to stop them, but I couldn't.

How could she tell him?

Had she? Or was he bluffing? I didn't know. And that was somehow worse.

I'd let her in—trusted her with the part of me I still didn't fully understand. And now it felt like that trust had shattered into a thousand pieces.

Not just betrayal.

Betrayal by the one person I thought would always protect me.

Chapter 14

I stepped off the city bus, legs unsteady, heart heavy. Jason's words still echoed sharply and cruelly, on a never-ending loop. The ride home had blurred by in fragments. Faces. Crosswalks. The hiss of brakes. None of it landed. I barely noticed the sidewalk beneath me, the wet path leading home coated in a film of slush. My foot slipped once, but I didn't care; I already felt like I was falling apart.

My mom's car was in the driveway.

I stopped short.

Panic tightened in my chest. Not tonight. Not after everything. I couldn't let her see me like this. Not when I'd been trying so hard to hold it together to keep things normal. She had enough on her plate without worrying whether her son was emotionally unraveling in public.

I scrubbed at my face, erasing tear tracks and panic with the sleeve of my hoodie, and forced myself forward.

The front door creaked under my hand. The warmth inside brushed against my skin, but it didn't reach the knot coiled in my chest. I stepped in quietly, already veering toward the stairs, hoping—foolishly—that maybe I could just disappear.

"Rion, is that you?" my mom called from the kitchen.

Her voice was casual, light, but I heard the edge under it.

I stopped, sighed, then called back the first thing that came to mind: "Nope. Just Luna looking for snacks."

My voice cracked slightly. The joke landed unevenly, like a plate wobbling on the edge of a table. Still, it was better than silence. Better than nothing.

She stepped into the hall, a dish towel slung over one shoulder, a streak of flour on her cheek like she'd wiped her face without realizing. Her bun was lopsided, and her smile started to form until she really looked at me. The smile dropped.

"Rion," she said, soft but sharp. "What's wrong?"

I raised my hands as if I could physically block the question. "It's nothing. Just tired. Rubbed my eyes too hard or something."

She didn't buy it. I could tell by the way her eyes narrowed, her mouth tightening just slightly. But she didn't push. Not yet.

"Okay," she said finally. "But before you disappear upstairs and ghost me all night, there's something on your bed. Early Christmas gift."

That caught me off guard.

"A present?"

She nodded, smile reappearing in full now. "Go check."

Curiosity sparked somewhere beneath the exhaustion. I walked the short hall to my room, footsteps muffled against the worn carpet. The moment I opened the door, everything else fell away.

Two brand-new Wilson Blade rackets sat on my bed.

I froze in disbelief.

The packaging was still crisp, untouched. The green-and-black frames gleamed under the soft yellow light. My jaw dropped.

It was the same racket I'd demoed. The same one Coach Moore had put in my hands a few weeks ago after practice.

"Try this," he'd said, tossing it to me like it wasn't worth more than my entire tennis wardrobe. "See how it feels."

I'd gripped the handle, instantly noticing the difference: lighter, more balanced, like it was built for speed but could still take a punch. The first serve I hit felt like slicing through the air.

I'd spent the next hour drilling with it, forehands, backhands, volleys, and for the first time, it felt like my body and my racket weren't fighting each other. My old one had been holding me back. I just hadn't realized it until that moment.

After practice, I handed it back reluctantly.

Coach gave me a knowing smile. "Night and day, right?"

I'd nodded, trying not to let myself want it too much.

Now, seeing that exact racket in my bag—brand new, mine— it didn't feel real. I ran my fingers along the grip, heart thudding. I never expected to own one. Not in a million years.

I reached out, fingers hovering like I might wake up if I touched it. When I finally picked one up, the weight settled into my palm like it had always belonged there. My breath caught. I hadn't realized how tight my chest had been until it eased, just slightly.

"She got me the set," I whispered, more to myself than anyone else.

I turned to Mom, still stunned. "How did you even...?"

She shrugged, like it was no big deal. "I've been setting a little aside every week. Didn't want to tell you until I was sure."

My throat tightened. I knew how tight things were. She worked double shifts, skipped lunches, drove a car that stalled in the cold. And still, she'd done this.

78

"I—I don't know what to say," I managed.

"You don't have to say anything." She smiled softly. "Just keep playing."

I didn't cry. Not really. But something cracked open inside me, just for a second. Because even when everything else felt like it was falling apart, she still saw me. Still believed in me. Still thought I was worth showing up for.

🎾🎾🎾

Later that night, while I was doomscrolling on Instagram, Sarah texted. I didn't respond to her last message.

What was there to say?

I wasn't even angry at Jason anymore. That was too easy. Too expected. But Sarah? She was supposed to know better. She did know better. She knew how private this was for me. How hard I was trying to hold onto control.

I didn't know if she told him directly or just let something slip, but it didn't matter. Either way, she opened the door. And Jason barged through it, grinning, smug, weaponizing it in front of a whole café.

And now he knew.

Which meant others would know too. Maybe not today. Maybe not even this week. But the clock was ticking.

I paced in my bedroom, phone in hand, new rackets in the other.

Sarah had been the one person I didn't guard myself against. The one person I'd trusted with the parts I couldn't even say out loud.

And she told him.

I stopped by the window, the glass cold against my palm. My

reflection stared back, red eyes, tight jaw. I didn't recognize myself.

I remembered the pinky promise we made in eighth grade. We were sitting under the bleachers, swearing we'd always be each other's people. No matter what. I'd believed her. God, I'd believed her.

Now I didn't know what to believe.

My phone buzzed.

Her name lit up the screen.

I'm sorry. I didn't think he'd figure it out. I never meant to hurt you.

The same apology. Over and over. Like saying sorry could rewind time.

I stared at it. My thumb hovered over the screen. One part of me still wanted to open the message. Still wanted to believe her.

My phone buzzed again. Sarah.

I didn't open it.

For a moment, I hovered, tempted. To forgive. To say something. To crack the door open.

But then I remembered the look on Jason's face when he said it. The smirk. The volume. The way he made it a joke. A spectacle.

I remembered how cold the air felt when I ran from the Honey Hive. How the tears froze against my skin.

I remembered not knowing who to blame, and hating that I had to blame her.

Tears came again. Quiet this time. No shaking. No breathless sobs. Just tears that fell and kept falling, even when I stopped trying to wipe them away.

Looking down at the phone, I hit delete.

Her number disappeared from my phone.

But not from my heart. The weight of her betrayal didn't vanish with the text. If anything, it settled deeper, pressing into the space where our friendship used to live.

Chapter 15

It had been almost two months since I deleted Sarah's number. Spring had arrived—painting the town in soft greens, blush-pink buds, and warm gold light. Everything looked fresh. Hopeful.

But inside, I still felt like winter.

I hadn't spoken to her since. Two months of dodging her at school, pretending not to notice when she was just a few feet away. Two months of radio silence between two people who used to talk about everything. The tension between us lingered like static in the air—quiet, charged, invisible to everyone else but loud in my bones.

At first, it wrecked me. Walking through school felt like walking through smoke—always on edge, expecting her to appear around the next corner, to say something. Anything. But I wasn't ready. Maybe I still wasn't. Every glimpse of her in the cafeteria, the library, the Honey Hive—it twisted in my chest like guilt and grief braided together.

So I shut it down. Stopped going to the Honey Hive altogether, at least for a while. But habits are hard to break. Once a week, I'd find myself back there, sipping my iced honey vanilla latte alone, tucked in a corner as far from our usual spot as I could get. I always told myself it'd be the last time.

It never was.

Some part of me—a stubborn, stupid part—kept hoping she'd show up too. That she missed me. That I wasn't the only one still hurting.

But today wasn't about any of that. Today was about tennis.

Tryouts were at 4:00 p.m.

And I was late.

Thanks to Sev, who conveniently "forgot" he was scheduled to work—I'd been stuck covering his shift at the club. By the time I checked the clock, I had twenty minutes to make it across town. Panic surged through me.

I made it onto the bus with seconds to spare, heart hammering. As soon as the doors hissed open in front of the school, I ran.

Sweat stung my eyes. My lungs ached. But I didn't stop. I couldn't.

The court was half-empty. A few players were packing up, laughter echoing through the space like a slow gut punch. My stomach dropped.

"Rion!"

Coach Konnor's voice rang out. He stood with his arms folded, his expression unreadable. "Why are you late?"

I didn't think. "Family emergency," I blurted, still panting. "Please... Coach. I need a chance. Tennis means everything to me."

A beat passed. His gaze didn't waver.

Then he gave a sharp nod. "One chance."

I could've collapsed with relief. "Thank you. I swear I won't waste it."

Coach clapped his hands, calling the rest of the players over. "Final tryout. Rion will face Greg in a 10-point tiebreaker. First to ten wins."

A buzz rippled through the gym. Greg, already half-packed, raised an eyebrow, then stood up and twirled his racket like this was a warm-up. I ground my teeth. Smug as ever.

Coach flipped a coin. "Call it."

"Heads."

It landed tails.

Of course.

Greg served first, sharp and clean, like he was born doing it. I returned it fast, backhand slicing clean. The ball snapped back and forth, a rhythm taking shape—serve, volley, rally. I locked in, breathing shallow, feet dancing across the court.

He was good. Captain good.

But I had something to prove.

Midway through a rally, I caught it—Greg shifting too far right. His stance opened just wide enough. I lunged left, drove the ball across the court, and landed the point.

"1-0, Rion," the Coach called.

I clenched my fist, adrenaline flooding my arms. Greg's jaw twitched as he tossed the ball back. He was rattled. Good.

The score climbed. 4-3. 6-5. 8-7.

And then—9-7.

Game point.

Greg stepped to the line, shoulders tight. The whole gym hushed. He served.

Right into the net.

A few players chuckled, but I didn't let it distract me. He re-set quickly. That meant he was nervous.

The serve came fast, but so did my swing.

I caught the corner, low and wide. Greg dove. Missed.

"Point, Rion."

Game.

For a second, I didn't move. Then I dropped to my knees and laughed, breathless and shaking.

Greg approached, sweat trickling down his brow, eyes sharp, but respectful.

"Welcome to the team," he said, clapping my shoulder.

Chapter 16

The air in the library smelled of old paper, ink, and something faintly musty, like the ghosts of long-forgotten stories. It was nearly empty, just a few students hunched over desks, their faces lit by the dull glow of laptop screens. The stillness pressed in, unnaturally quiet for someone like me, whose thoughts were never still.

I'd never been a library person, not because I hated reading, but because the silence always made my head too loud. Still, I was there, pulled in by some weird urge to disappear for a while. To drift between shelves, between other people's stories, and forget my own.

The town library felt too big for our small town. Endless rows of books stretched out like mazes, making the space feel vast and hollow. I wandered past them slowly, bag slung over one shoulder, scanning spines without reading a single title. I didn't know what I was looking for, maybe nothing. Maybe quiet. Maybe answers.

My sneakers squeaked on the wooden floor, too loud in the silence, as if the library didn't want me there. I smirked at the thought. I knocked over a shelf and causing a domino disaster. It was dumb, but the image made me laugh under my breath. Anything to break the quiet.

I turned down another row, heading toward the science section.

Then I stopped cold.

Even from several feet away, I recognized those wild auburn curls.

Sarah.

She stood two shelves down, flipping through a book with a fake interest that screamed distraction. But it wasn't her that made my stomach twist.

It was who she was standing with. Ashley.

Seeing them together didn't make sense. Sarah hated Ashley. They barely acknowledged each other, and when they did, it was never civil. But here they were, side by side in the science aisle as if this were normal. Like I wasn't watching a scene from a parallel universe.

I ducked behind a nearby shelf, heart thudding, pressing my back against the dusty wood. I wasn't proud of it, but I wasn't ready to face either of them. Not after everything.

I peeked through a small gap in the books, just in time to catch Ashley stepping closer, her voice low but sharp.

"You must think pretty highly of yourself, Sarah."

Sarah straightened. I couldn't see her expression clearly, but her voice was clipped and tight. "I don't have time for this. What do you want?"

Ashley's lips curled into something smug. "Glad you asked. Stay away from Jason."

The words slammed into me.

Jason. Of course.

Sarah's voice faltered. "What do you mean?"

"Stay away from him," Ashley repeated, crossing her arms. "He's not into you. He never was. You're just a filler. A plot

87

twist. Jason and I," she paused, flipping her hair like she was in a teen drama, "are meant to be."

The venom in her voice made my skin crawl. I clenched my fists at my sides.

Ashley didn't stop. "You think just because he kissed you a few times it means something? Please. He's just using you to stir up drama between you and Rion, between everyone. You're a distraction."

I couldn't see Sarah's face, but I could hear the disbelief in her silence.

Ashley's tone sharpened like a blade.

"Let's be real, Sarah. You don't belong in our world. You're a science geek with a messy ponytail and hand-me-down boots. You really think Jason's going to bring you home to his mom?"

My chest tightened. I hated her, hated how easily she said those words, how calmly she dismantled someone with a smile.

Sarah's voice cut through the tension—quiet, but firm. "If I'm so beneath him, why hasn't he dumped me?"

Ashley smirked, eyes gleaming. "Maybe he's bored. Or maybe he just hasn't figured out how to let you down easy."

I could feel Sarah becoming tense. Her knuckles were white around the strap of her bag, but she held her ground.

Ashley tilted her head, voice dripping with mock sympathy. "Come on, Sarah. You think someone like Jason ends up with someone like you? His family throws fundraisers for politicians. And who knows what your parents do."

That landed like a slap. The words hung heavy in the air, money, class, worth. Like, Sarah wasn't just dating the wrong guy, she was trespassing.

Sarah stood straighter. "Maybe his mom throws parties, but Jason still wanted me. He chose me."

Ashley laughed, low and cold. "For now."

Then Ashley scoffed. "You're delusional," she said.

Sarah didn't flinch. "Maybe. But at least I don't throw tantrums in the library like a small child."

Ashley's face turned crimson. She spun on her heel and stormed off, heels clicking violently across the floor until the front doors snapped shut behind her.

Silence returned.

Sarah stood alone in the aisle, one hand still clutched around the spine of a book. She wasn't shaking, but I could see the effort it took to stay upright. I knew that look, holding yourself together because if you didn't, you might fall apart.

And for the first time in months, I didn't feel angry at her.

I felt protective.

I'd spent so long resenting her for what happened—what she told Jason, how it got out, but seeing her now, standing against someone like Ashley with zero backup? It chipped away at my wall. She looked so... alone.

Maybe I'd been wrong to push her away completely. Maybe not everything was as black-and-white as I made it out to be.

I hovered in the shadows, watching her gather herself before quietly slipping out of the aisle.

I stayed hidden. My legs didn't move.

When I finally left the library, the spring air smelled of spring flowers and wet pavement. The sun filtered through clouds, soft and gold, like the town had been waiting to exhale.

But I couldn't shake the image of Sarah standing there, fire in her voice, tremble in her hands.

Maybe our friendship wasn't dead. Just buried.

Chapter 17

I sat alone in the cafeteria every day now, just like today. Sarah had been the only person I ever ate with, and without her, everything felt quieter, hollower. I poked at the meatloaf with my fork, cutting it into perfect little pieces I had no intention of eating. It tasted like cardboard dipped in regret. I didn't even know why I still bothered with school lunches. Habit, maybe. Or hope.

I stood up to throw my tray out, trying to block out the cafeteria noise, buzzing voices, chair legs scraping tile, the occasional slamming locker from down the hall. It all bled together, one big white noise machine. But even in the chaos, I could hear them.

Jason's voice rose above the rest like a siren I couldn't ignore. That fake laugh. That smug swagger as he walked through the crowd with his usual group of followers, all empty words and oversized egos. And then—he locked eyes with me.

My stomach dropped. I looked away, but it didn't matter. He was already walking toward me.

He didn't say anything at first. Just stood there with that awful grin, like he'd already decided how this was going to go. And then, without warning, he cracked open his milk carton and dumped it over my head.

Cold soaked through my hair, my hoodie, my jeans. It ran down my neck and into my shoes. I sat there stunned, shivering, my tray still in my hands as milk pooled around my sneakers. I didn't move.

For a second, it was quiet.

Then the laughter came.

Explosive. Cruel. Loud enough to echo. Jason's friends practically fell over themselves, high-fiving and howling like they'd just witnessed the peak of comedy.

But something inside me shifted. Snapped.

I stood up—slow, shaking, dripping—but taller than I'd felt in weeks.

"You think that was funny?" My voice didn't shake. It cut through the room like ice. "You think being a bully makes you important? It doesn't. It makes you a coward."

Jason's grin twitched.

"You spend so much time trying to humiliate other people, it's almost sad. Almost. But mostly it's just pathetic. Because deep down, you know the truth—nobody actually likes you, Jason. They're just afraid you'll turn on them next."

His smirk faltered. His friends went quiet.

I wasn't done.

"You act like you're better than everyone, but all you are is loud and miserable. You use people. You break them down so you don't have to deal with whatever garbage you've got bottled up inside. And guess what? It's not working. You're still miserable. You're still small."

Jason looked around like he was waiting for someone to save him. No one moved.

"You want to dump milk on someone? Go ahead. That's all you've got, milk cartons and cheap shots. Meanwhile, I've got

91

an actual future. You? You've peaked here."

He didn't say a word. Not a single comeback. His face was stone, but his eyes were different now. They weren't smug anymore. They were angry. Embarrassed. Scared.

Good.

I dropped my tray, letting the splattered food hit the floor next to the puddle of milk. And then I walked out.

Past his friends. Past the silence. Out into the hallway, where the air felt sharp and clean.

I didn't cry. I didn't scream.

I just kept walking.

Finally, I could breathe.

🎾🎾🎾

After school, I headed to the Honey Hive. The place was quiet, warm. I took my usual spot by the window, pulled out my textbooks, and opened to the first page. My hands were still trembling.

A few minutes later, a soft thud landed on my table. I looked up to see Shawn standing there, a cup of mocha with whipped cream in his hand. He set it down with a grin.

"It's on the house," he said, ruffling my hair. "Can I sit?"

"Yeah, sure," I replied, feeling a warmth spread through me that had nothing to do with the coffee.

Shawn pulled out the chair across from me and sat, his eyes locking onto mine like always, like he could see straight through me.

"What?" I asked, squirming under his gaze.

He shrugged, leaning back. "I've just been wondering, why do you care about tennis so much?

92

The question caught me off guard. I paused. "Same reason you're into baking," I said with a shrug.

He chuckled, but I could tell he actually wanted to know.

"Tennis has been a part of my life since I was a kid. My idols, Serena and Venus, they're the reason I picked up a racket in the first place. Watching them play gave me a sense of purpose. They're not just talented, they've overcome so much, and they never quit. I guess tennis became my way of feeling like I could do something important too."

Shawn nodded, his expression softening. "That's cool," he said, voice low. "I get it. Everyone needs something that makes them feel alive."

We sat in an easy silence. For the first time in a while, I felt like I could breathe.

He glanced out the window, then back at me, his grin widening.

"How about you give me a lesson sometime? I've never played tennis before."

I laughed. "You want me to teach you?"

"Why not?" he said, leaning forward with a glint in his eye. "You said you're passionate about it. Share the love."

I couldn't help but smile. "Alright, fine. How about a private lesson tomorrow at the school courts? No pressure, just for fun."

"Deal," Shawn said, bumping his fist against mine.

The next day after school, we met at the tennis courts. The spring air was crisp, the sun beginning to set and cast a golden light over the court. Shawn showed up in casual clothes, holding a borrowed racket and looking a little unsure.

"You ready?" I asked, bouncing on the balls of my feet. I was more excited than I expected.

"I have no idea what I'm doing," Shawn said with a grin. "But yeah, let's do this."

We started with the basics, how to hold the racket, the proper stance, how to swing. Shawn picked things up quickly, his natural athleticism showing even though he'd never played before. Soon, we were rallying back and forth, the sound of the ball hitting our rackets filling the air.

"You're getting the hang of it," I said after a particularly good volley.

"Maybe I'm just a natural," he teased, wiping sweat from his forehead.

We collapsed onto the court, sitting side by side as we caught our breath. The sun dipped lower, shadows stretching across the court. The air felt cool against my skin.

I glanced over at Shawn. We sat close enough for our arms to brush, and even though we were both winded, I felt strangely calm.

"So," Shawn said after a moment, "what's going on with Sarah?"

The question caught me off guard. A lump rose in my throat.

"I don't know," I admitted, my voice low. "Things were... complicated."

Shawn nodded, waiting for me to continue. I stared at the ground, trying to find the right words.

"She outed me to Jason," I said, my voice cracking. "She just... told him. And he used it against me. I couldn't forgive her for that."

Shawn didn't say anything at first. When he spoke, his voice was soft. "That's rough. I can't imagine how that felt."

I nodded, tears pressing at the corners of my eyes. "I trusted her, you know? And she betrayed me."

Without another word, Shawn pulled me into a hug. His arms were warm and steady. For a moment, I let myself relax into it, the weight on my chest lifting, if only briefly.

When we pulled apart, I looked at him, really looked at him. His eyes were soft, filled with understanding, and something else I couldn't name. My heart thudded, loud and uncertain. And before I could stop myself, I leaned in and kissed him.

For a second, everything felt still, then it shattered.

Shawn's hands gently pushed me away. His expression was full of confusion and apology.

"Rion," he said softly, "I... I'm sorry, but I'm..."

My heart cracked open, sharp and sudden. I stumbled back, not allowing him to finish speaking, my face burning. Without another word, I grabbed my bag and ran, leaving Shawn and everything I'd just risked behind.

Chapter 18

The next morning, I lay in bed, staring at the ceiling, the light from the blinds cutting golden stripes across my room. But I couldn't feel the warmth. My mind was a storm, raging, restless.

I kissed Shawn.

My stomach flipped all over again. My chest knotted, tight with regret. Not because I didn't want to kiss him, I did. Every part of me had screamed to do it. But now, every part of me screamed, *Why did you do that?*

He didn't kiss me back. He didn't even flinch. He *pushed me away.*

I buried my face in the pillow, the sting of rejection burning hot behind my eyes. It wasn't supposed to be like that. This was my first kiss, and was supposed to mean something. It was supposed to feel like a beginning, not an ending. Not like this.

The shame clung to me like a second skin. The image of his hands gently pushing me away played on repeat. His voice soft, apologetic, like he pitied me.

Why did I ruin everything?

Tears spilled out before I could stop them. I pressed my face deeper into the pillow, wishing I could melt into it. Disappear. Be anyone else but the boy who kissed the wrong person at the worst time.

A knock on my door interrupted the spiral.

"Rion, breakfast," Mom called through the hallway, her voice light and oblivious.

I swallowed hard. Wiped my eyes on my pillow. I couldn't let her see me like this, not cracked open. Not after everything.

"Okay, coming," I said, the words barely louder than a breath.

Dragging myself out of bed felt like wading through mud. I moved slowly—robotic—washing my face, brushing my teeth, splashing cold water on my cheeks. None of it helped.

The smell of bacon and eggs met me at the top of the stairs. Normally, it would've been comforting. Today, it just made me feel heavy.

Mom was at the table, coffee in hand, humming something I didn't recognize. She looked up as I walked in, smiling like the world hadn't tilted on its axis the night before.

"Morning, sweetie. Sleep okay?"

"Yeah. Fine," I muttered, dropping into the seat across from her. I poked at the eggs like they were some kind of puzzle I had to solve.

She sipped her coffee and watched me for a second longer than felt casual.

Silence.

"So," she said finally, too casually, "I haven't seen Sarah around in a while."

My fork froze mid-air.

Of course, she'd ask.

"She's fine," I said, quickly. "Busy with tutoring and stuff."

Mom tilted her head. "You two used to be attached at the hip. Everything okay?"

I nodded, eyes locked on my plate. "Yep. Totally fine."

The lie hit my tongue like ash. I didn't even know how to explain what had happened with Sarah anymore. All I had were broken pieces, guilt, confusion, betrayal. Was I mad at her? Did I miss her? Did I hate her for what happened? Or myself for not letting it go?

Mom didn't press, but I saw it in her eyes, questions she wasn't ready to ask out loud. She changed the subject.

"How's tennis going? You've been busy with lessons at the country club, huh?"

I nodded automatically. "Yeah. It's fine. I've gotten used to the kitchen routine."

I stopped.

"Kitchen routine?" She asked with an inquisitive tone.

I looked up. Her brow furrowed. Her mug froze halfway to her lips.

"What kitchen routine?" she said slowly, setting the mug down.

Panic flared in my chest. I scrambled.

"Oh—uh—the kitchen staff. I just meant I've gotten to know them. I pass through there sometimes. They showed me how stuff works."

She blinked. "You pass through the kitchen?"

I shrugged. "Yeah. I'm always there. Makes sense."

She didn't look convinced, but she didn't press.

Then her mouth twitched into a smile. "And how's Shawn?"

I almost choked on my orange juice.

"What?"

She tried to hide a grin. "You've been spending a lot of time with him there lately. Just wondering."

My heart thudded. She knew. Or at least, thought she knew.

Chapter 19

Monday slammed into me. I woke with a pounding headache, like the past few weeks had finally caught up with me, and decided to settle behind my eyes. It had been months since I deleted Sarah's number, and I'd done everything I could to avoid her at school, at the Honey Hive, everywhere. But no matter how hard I tried to block her out, our friendship clung to me like a ghost, appearing in every quiet moment, every silent walk to class. I missed her, but forgiving her still felt like too much.

I rolled out of bed, rubbing my temples, and shuffled to the bathroom. By the time I made it to the kitchen, Mom was already at the table with her coffee. She looked up, concern flickering across her face.

"Morning, sweetie. You sleep okay?" she asked, voice soft and probing.

I grabbed a piece of toast and forced a smile. "Yeah. Fine."

She watched me a beat too long, like she was scanning for cracks. I focused on buttering my toast, avoiding her eyes.

"I gotta catch the bus, or I'll be late," I said quickly, dodging any deeper questions.

The bus ride was quiet. I sat by the window, letting the gray sky smear into the passing streets. My thoughts spiraled, looping around the same ache: Shawn. The kiss. The silence since. I'd probably ruined that too.

When we finally pulled up to school, I stepped into the cold morning air and shoved my hands deep into my pockets. Spring hadn't fully shaken the chill yet. The wind cut right through me.

Something felt off the moment I walked inside.

There was a strange buzz in the hallway, a low murmur that moved like static through the crowd. I scanned the corridor, heart already bracing.

Then I saw it.

Flyers. Hundreds of them. Plastered on lockers, taped to walls, hanging crooked from bulletin boards. And every single one had the same thing printed in thick, black type above a grainy photo of my face:

RION MILLER IS QUEER.

Time stopped. My breath caught. My stomach turned inside out. The words burned themselves into my brain like they'd been branded there. I tore one off the nearest locker, hands shaking.

Laughter. Whispers. Eyes. All on me.

Snickering from behind. Stares from in front. My skin felt like it was peeling under their gazes.

Jason.

Of course, it was Jason. After the cafeteria? I should've seen this coming. But this... this was next-level cruelty. Premeditated. Public. Meant to humiliate, not just scare.

I tore down every flyer I passed, the paper shredding under my fingers. I didn't care how it looked. I didn't care who was watching. I just needed them gone.

And I needed to find him.

I knew where he'd be, always too cocky to hide.

I stormed down the hall toward Mr. Saltzman. classroom. The door was open a crack. Inside, I heard his voice, casual, smug.

But then another voice cut in.

Sarah.

I froze mid-step.

Peering through the gap, I saw her, standing in front of Jason, fists clenched, her face flushed with fury. Students lingered behind her near the lockers, silent and stunned, their eyes bouncing between the two like it was a live boxing match.

"Just how low can you go, Jason?" she snapped. "I told you something by accident, and you turned it into a joke for the whole school? You're disgusting."

Jason leaned back against a desk, arms crossed. "Oh, come on, Sarah. It's a joke. You're seriously this pressed about it?"

She didn't back down. She stepped closer. Her voice dropped but sharpened.

"This isn't a joke. It's his life. And you're trashing it because you can't stand the fact that he stood up to you after you poured milk on him in front of the entire cafeteria."

Jason stood. He was taller, broader, but Sarah didn't flinch.

"You know what?" he said, his voice venomous. "Maybe I wouldn't be so insecure if my girlfriend wasn't always crawling to defend her little gay best friend."

The words hit like a punch. The breath whooshed out of me. My fists curled, shaking.

But Sarah was faster.

Her hand cracked across his face, so hard the room went silent.

Jason's head whipped to the side. He staggered a step. His

cheek flamed red.

"We're done," she said, voice like ice. "Don't come near me or Rion again." She spun on her heel, storming out as the crowd parted.

Her eyes caught mine in the hallway. I froze, still half-hidden by the lockers.

She didn't say anything, just kept moving toward the nearest wall of flyers. Her hands ripped them down in handfuls, tearing fast, like the paper might burn her if she stopped.

I moved without thinking, walking toward her. She didn't look up until I gently grabbed her wrist.

"Sarah, wait."

She turned to me, eyes wet but steady. Her voice cracked as she spoke.

"Rion, I'm so sorry. For everything. For telling Jason. For not thinking. For betraying you. I was scared, and stupid, and I hurt you. And now this... this mess, it's all my fault."

She couldn't hold it in. Her shoulders trembled, her words tumbling over themselves.

"I didn't mean to ruin us. I didn't mean to let him do this to you. I was just, I didn't know what to do."

Part of me wanted to pull away. To hold onto the anger that had protected me for months. But I couldn't.

She had stood up for me. Publicly and fiercely. When I needed someone the most, she chose me. Again.

I looked at her, and in her face, I saw not just guilt, but grief. She'd lost me too.

I took a shaky breath.

"I'm still mad," I admitted. "Still hurt. But... I forgive you."

Her eyes widened, and I pulled her into a hug. She clung to me like she hadn't breathed in weeks.

"I missed you," she whispered.

"I missed you too."

We stood like that for a long moment, surrounded by scraps of torn paper. Students passed by, some watching, some pretending not to, but I didn't care. Not this time.

Eventually, we stepped back. She sniffled and gave me a small, grateful smile.

"I'll help you take them down," she said.

So we did, side by side, down the hallway, pulling down every last flyer like we were reclaiming something stolen.

The tension didn't vanish completely. Jason was still at school. My feelings for Shawn still hadn't left. And I didn't know where anything stood with him, scared I ruined a growing friendship. But with Sarah at my side again, the weight didn't crush me.

Chapter 20

The sun dipped low on the horizon, casting long shadows over the tennis court as I pushed through another round of footwork drills. My legs burned with each shuffle, sprint, and pivot, muscles screaming in protest. Sweat trickled down my forehead, stinging my eyes. Still, I kept moving. Coach Moore had drilled it into me: footwork was the foundation of every strong game. Unfortunately, it was also my weakest part.

I paused, bending forward with my hands on my hips, trying to catch my breath. The school grounds had emptied, leaving behind a silence broken only by the distant hum of traffic and the occasional chirp of birds. The stillness was unsettling, like the calm before something I couldn't name.

Just as I reached for my water bottle, the back doors of the school banged open. I looked up and spotted Sarah walking toward me, arms loaded with books. Her wild hair caught the last of the fading sunlight, giving her a kind of soft glow that felt oddly nostalgic. For a second, it was like nothing had changed, like we were just two friends meeting after school, same as always.

"Come on, Miller! Move those feet!" she called, her voice playful and teasing, echoing across the court.

I laughed, shaking my head. "Let's see you run some of these drills, then."

"Whatever, Rion," she replied with a grin, balancing her stack as she made her way over. "I'll leave the tennis to you. I've got enough going on with this U.S. History test. You know, real stress."

I bent down to stretch. "And how many textbooks does it take to stress you out? You look like you're training for the Academic Olympics."

Sarah shrugged dramatically as she reached the bench. She dropped the books with a soft thud and brushed a strand of hair behind her ear. "You always say I overprepare. I just don't want to bomb the final while you're off becoming the next tennis prodigy."

"Sarah, I've known you basically my whole life. I don't think you've ever bombed anything," I said, grabbing my water bottle for a long swig.

She flipped open one of the textbooks and settled in, and just like that, it felt easy again. Familiar.

"Yeah, yeah. Keep the praise coming, Coach Miller," she said in her best imitation of Coach Moore's gruff tone. She leaned back, her eyes scanning the court. "You actually don't look half bad out there, you know."

I gave her a theatrical bow and wiped the sweat from my forehead. "Big words from someone whose only workout is carrying textbooks."

"Hey, I'm multitasking," she said, raising an eyebrow. "I'm here to quiz you while you train. Two birds. One stone."

"Oh joy," I muttered, picking up my racket. "Let me guess, history?"

"Of course," she said, already flipping through flashcards. "You want to pass, don't you? Okay, who wrote the Declaration of Independence?"

I slid into position. "Thomas Jefferson. Next."

She flipped to the next card. "What battle turned the tide of the American Revolution?"

"Saratoga."

"Correct." She smirked. "Looks like your extra studying is finally kicking in."

As I moved through drills, Sarah kept the questions coming. Her voice was steady, and something about the rhythm of her quizzing and the thud of my feet on the court made everything feel less heavy, like the world was tilting back toward normal.

When I finished the last drill, I collapsed onto the bench beside her, legs on fire, lungs burning. She handed me a towel and a bottle of water, her grin still playful.

"Not bad, Miller. I think you've officially earned the right not to flunk history."

I muttered a half-laugh, leaning back on the bench. A breeze rolled across the court, coming from the open door on the side of the tennis bubble, cool against my sweaty skin. The peace of the moment settled over me, but there was a weight still clinging to my chest, unspoken, unresolved.

Shawn's face drifted through my mind, his expression after I kissed him. The confusion. The apology. The rejection.

I stared at the sky, trying to clear my head, but it wasn't working.

"Sarah..." I said, quieter than I intended. "There's something I need to tell you."

She looked up from her notes, her expression instantly serious. "What's up?"

I hesitated, my fingers tightening around the handle of my racket. "Remember last week, when I said things with Shawn were... weird?"

She nodded slowly. "Yeah. What happened?"

I blew out a breath, then scratched the back of my neck. "I kissed him."

Her eyes widened. For a second, she just blinked at me.

Then she burst out laughing—loud and completely unfiltered. "Wait. You kissed my brother?!"

I groaned, dropping my face into my hands. "Not funny."

"No, I mean, okay, I'm sorry," she said through her laughter, wiping at her eyes. "It's just... wow. I didn't see that coming."

I peeked through my fingers. "Yeah. Well, it didn't go great. He pushed me away."

Her expression shifted in an instant. "Seriously?"

I nodded, the knot in my chest tightening. "I don't know what I was thinking. I just... I felt something. It felt right in the moment. But clearly, it wasn't."

Sarah went quiet, her lips pressing into a thoughtful line. "Okay... but for what it's worth, Shawn's been weird lately too. Asking about you. A lot."

I frowned. "Like what?"

She shrugged. "Just... little things. How you're doing. What you've been up to. At first, I thought it was just because we weren't talking, but now? Maybe he was figuring something out."

My heart did a weird flip. "You think he might like me?"

She gave a small, lopsided smile. "Wouldn't shock me. You're kind of a catch, you know."

I blinked. "Wait. Did you actually just call me a catch?"

She rolled her eyes. "Don't let it go to your head."

Her tone softened. "Look, Rion... I know I messed things up between us. But I've been doing a lot of thinking. I never want to make you feel like you have to hide any part of yourself again."

Her words hit hard. They cracked something open in me, something I hadn't realized I was still holding onto.

"Thank you," I said quietly. "That means more than you know."

We sat together for a long while after that. The floodlights buzzed faintly behind us, casting pale light over the court, but the world felt calm. Balanced.

Things still weren't perfect. There was still Shawn, still school, still stuff I hadn't figured out. But for the first time in weeks, I wasn't carrying it alone.

Chapter 21

Saturday morning started like any other. I was groggy, disoriented, and painfully reluctant to open my eyes.

My alarm blared from across the room, screaming at me to get up. I buried my face deeper into the pillow, wishing I could turn it off with my mind.

My legs felt like concrete, still sore from the footwork drills from the night before. My whole body ached like I'd run a marathon. Maybe if I lay there long enough, the day would disappear, and I wouldn't have to move.

But of course, the alarm didn't care about my aching legs or my desperate need for sleep. It just kept going. Relentless.

I groaned, reached out blindly to kill the noise, then rolled onto my back and stared at the ceiling.

Five minutes went by. Then ten. Before I knew it, I had spent twenty minutes scrolling aimlessly through Instagram, liking random posts without even looking at them.

I should have gotten up. I really should have.

A text notification popped up on my screen. I glanced at it lazily. It was from Sally.

My heart stopped. Panic shot through me like lightning. I didn't even open it. I already knew.

I was late.

I leapt out of bed, tossed my phone onto the blankets, and scrambled to find my work uniform.

My room was a disaster, clothes everywhere, textbooks piled on the desk, an empty pizza box in the corner. Of course, my uniform was nowhere to be found.

"Shit, shit, shit," I muttered, frantically digging under the bed.

My hands found the uniform shirt. I'd hidden under there so my mom wouldn't find it. I yanked it out and crammed the rest of the uniform into my backpack without bothering to fold it. I was already running out of time.

I dashed out of my room, nearly tripping over a sneaker, and sprinted down the hall toward the kitchen.

Mom was at the table, sipping coffee and flipping through the newspaper, her usual Saturday routine. She looked up as I raced past, grabbing a Pop-Tart from the cabinet.

"Rion, wait," she started.

"Running late for practice! Bye!" I shouted, cramming the Pop-Tart into my mouth as I bolted for the door.

"Rion, we need to talk," she called after me, but I was already halfway out.

The cool morning air hit me like a slap as I sprinted to the bus stop, heart pounding. I fumbled for my phone and quickly texted Sally: *On my way. Be there soon.*

A few seconds later, she replied: *Okay, but everyone's on edge because of the wedding today. I'll try to cover for you.*

Of course. The one day, I was late there's a massive wedding at the country club. Just my luck.

By the time the bus pulled up, I was a sweaty, out-of-breath mess. I sprinted across the parking lot, weaving between cars, clutching my backpack, and trying not to trip.

I burst through the kitchen's back door, gasping, face flushed.

The kitchen buzzed with clanging pots and shouted orders from the chefs. I slipped into the corner and grabbed a fresh serving apron, hoping no one would notice how late I was.

But before I could catch my breath, I heard the unmistakable click-clack of heels on the tile.

I looked up just in time to see Jasmin, the head event planner, sweep through the kitchen like a hurricane in a pencil skirt. Sally and Chen trailed behind her, both scribbling furiously notes.

Jasmin didn't stop, but her voice dripped with sarcasm as she passed.

"Thanks for coming in today, Rion," she said without looking at me. "You'll be on kitchen duty all night."

Sally glanced over her shoulder and mouthed, *Sorry*, as she rushed to keep up.

I slumped against the counter, groaning.

Kitchen duty. All night. This is what I get for being late. Again.

I dragged myself to the dish station, already dreading the hours ahead. The sink overflowed with plates, silverware, and pots, all caked in gunk, and waiting for me. This was going to suck.

As I started scrubbing, sounds from the main hall drifted in, laughter, clinking glasses, soft music. One of those over-the-top weddings where everything had to be flawless, or Jasmin would spiral into full meltdown mode.

I attacked a crusted stain on a plate, my arms already sore, and trying not to count the hours left.

Halfway through the pile, Chen breezed in, apron crooked, hair falling out of the bun she'd failed to tame. She wiped her forehead and shook her head like she'd just escaped a warzone.

111

"How's it going, dish boy?" she said, grabbing a clean plate and giving me a quick, sympathetic smile.

"Oh, you know. Living the dream," I muttered, scrubbing harder. "How's the wedding?"

"Stressful," she said, leaning against the counter. "Jasmin's been barking orders all night. Sally and I are drowning. At least you're safe back here, though, right?"

I rolled my eyes. "Yeah. Really safe. Just me and these never-ending dishes."

Chen chuckled, grabbed a towel, and started drying plates. "Look on the bright side, at least you didn't have to deal with the bridezilla meltdown. She tried to change the seating chart last minute. Total chaos."

"Sounds like a nightmare," I said, glad for the distraction. "At least you're not stuck in here with Sev."

As if on cue, Sev sauntered into the kitchen, apron spotless, his usual cocky grin plastered in place.

"Speaking of nightmares..." He winked at Sally, then turned to me. "How's dish duty treating you, Miller?"

I gave an exaggerated sigh. "Oh, just fabulous. Living the dream over here."

Sev laughed and leaned against the counter. "Well, if it makes you feel any better, I had to deal with a drunk groomsmen who thought it'd be funny to start a food fight during cocktail hour. So, you know, it could be worse."

"Sure, keep telling yourself that," I muttered, tossing a clean plate onto the drying rack.

The three of us chatted for a bit, trading war stories from the night. For a few minutes, it actually felt fun. But soon enough, Sally and Sev and Chen got pulled back into the fray, leaving me alone with my mountain of dishes.

The hours dragged on. The pile of dirty plates like it would never end. Eventually, the noise from the event began to die down, replaced by faint music and quiet goodbyes. The wedding was winding down, and with it, my shift was finally ending.

When the last dish was finally clean, I slumped against the counter and wiped the sweat from my forehead. My arms felt like jelly, my back ached, and my feet were killing me, but it was over. I untied my apron and tossed it in the laundry bin, relief mixing with exhaustion as it hit me all at once.

The staff trickled out of the club, and I followed them to the employee lot, my backpack slung over one shoulder. The night air was cool after the heat of the kitchen. I breathed it in deep, my muscles relaxing for the first time all day.

As I headed for the bus stop, a car horn honked behind me. Sally's beat-up sedan pulled up to the curb, the passenger window rolling down.

"Need a ride?" she said with a grin.

I hesitated, glancing down the street at the bus stop, then nodded, too tired to care. "Yeah, thanks."

I climbed into the passenger seat, dropping my backpack at my feet as Sally pulled away from the curb. The ride home was quiet, both of us too drained to talk much, but the silence between us felt easy. Comfortable.

Moments like this reminded me that I wasn't really alone. Even after chaos, I had people who had my back.

When we finally pulled up to my house, I gave Sally a tired smile. "Thanks for the ride."

"Anytime, Miller," she said, waving as I climbed out. "See you at the next disaster."

I laughed, shut the door, and watched her taillights fade into the night.

Turning toward the house, I felt the weight of the day settle on me, but underneath it, tucked between the exhaustion and the ache, was a strange flicker of pride. I'd made it through.

Chapter 22

The house stood in front of me, warm light spilling from the living room windows. I stood on the front step for a second longer than usual, staring at the glow like it was unfamiliar. All I wanted was to collapse in bed and forget about the chaos of the day, but something about the stillness made me uneasy. Like the house was waiting for me to face something I wasn't ready for.

I stepped inside. The scent of dinner greeted me immediately, something warm and home-cooked, like roasted chicken with garlic mashed potatoes. My stomach growled, a sharp reminder that I hadn't eaten anything real since that morning's sad excuse for a Pop-Tart.

I kicked off my shoes and stretched, every muscle protesting. My legs were still sore from drills the day before. My arms ached from dish duty, and my brain was foggy with exhaustion. School, tennis, work. It was all starting to blur together. I could feel the cracks widening beneath me, but I kept pretending everything was fine.

The living room light flickered.

Just as I turned toward the hallway, my mom's voice floated in from the next room.

"Rion, come in here."

The way she said it, calm, low, but unmistakably serious, sent a jolt through me. Not angry. Not tired. But something in between, like she already knew what I didn't want her to. My stomach dropped.

I forced a smile, the kind I'd gotten good at faking, and walked into the living room.

She sat on the couch, arms crossed, her mouth set in a tight line. Her eyes found mine the second I stepped in. There was no trace of warmth in them, just quiet disappointment. That was worse than yelling. So much worse.

"Hey, Mom," I said, keeping my tone light. Casual. Normal. "What's up?"

She didn't answer right away. Just studied me. "Why don't you tell me how tennis practice went today?"

My heart skipped. Crap.

"Uh... it was good," I said, shifting my weight, trying not to sound rehearsed. "Coach had us doing footwork drills. Still trying to fix my foot speed, you know?"

I smiled, even threw in a small chuckle.

She didn't smile back.

"Really?" she said, arching an eyebrow. "That's interesting."

The silence between us expanded. I could feel it pressing in on my chest. Her gaze flicked to the side, and for the first time, I noticed it, my tennis bag sitting on the couch beside her, unzipped. Exposed.

Something inside me snapped taut.

"You sure you're remembering it right?" she asked softly, voice calm, but her eyes said otherwise.

I opened my mouth. Nothing came out.

Then she reached for something on the side table. A folded paper.

"I found this in the laundry." She unfolded it and held it up. My pay stub. The world stopped.

My throat dried out. My brain scrambled for excuses, but none of them felt strong enough to hold up against the truth sitting in her hand.

"I know about your job at the country club," she said. "How long were you planning to keep that from me?"

She didn't raise her voice. That made it worse. Her calmness felt like something sharp in disguise. She wasn't just disappointed, she was hurt. And she was trying not to show it.

"I—" I tried again, my voice catching. "I can explain."

"I'm listening," she said, leaning back but never breaking eye contact. Her arms stayed crossed protective, closed off.

I sank down onto the arm chair across from her, resting my elbows on my knees. The fatigue I'd been ignoring all day suddenly hit me like a wave.

"I took the job because I didn't want you to worry about paying for my tennis lessons," the words spilling out, raw and unfiltered. "They kept getting more expensive. I saw the bills. I knew it was stressing you out."

Her face softened slightly, but her jaw stayed clenched.

"I thought if I worked there, I could help cover it," I continued. "And the club gives discounts to employees, so it made sense. I just... didn't want to put more on you."

She was quiet for a long moment.

"You've been working there for months," she finally said. "Lying every day. Pretending you were at practice when you weren't. Do you know how hard it is to find out from a piece of paper?"

I lowered my gaze. The shame hit hard.

"I'm sorry, Mom. I thought I could handle it."

She rubbed her forehead like she was trying to press away a headache. "I'm proud that you want to help. I really am. But what hurts is that you didn't trust me enough to tell me. You just shut me out."

"I wasn't trying to shut you out," I said, my voice small. "I just... I didn't want you to feel like you had to fix everything alone."

"I'm your mother. That's my job."

She uncrossed her arms and leaned forward. "You can't keep working there."

I sat up straighter. "But..."

"No, Rion," she said, more firmly. "You're overworked, your grades are slipping, you look exhausted all the time. And now you're hiding things. That's not okay. You're not an adult. You shouldn't have to carry this."

"But it's not just about the money," I said, my voice rising a little. "I like working there. I've made friends. I feel useful, like I'm actually doing something."

Her expression softened again. "And that's good. I want you to feel independent. But not at the cost of your health. Or your honesty. You're still a kid, Rion. You're allowed to lean on me."

That hit hard.

I hadn't let myself lean on anyone in a long time. Not really. I'd gotten used to being the one holding it all together, even when I wasn't. Even when I was breaking inside.

I exhaled, and for the first time in what felt like weeks, I let my guard fall just a little.

"Okay," I said, my voice cracking. "I'll quit."

She reached for my hand and squeezed it. "Thank you."

There was a pause. Then, softer, "I'm not angry. I'm just sad you thought you had to handle it all alone."

Tears welled up in my eyes. I blinked them back.

"I love you, Mom," I whispered.

"I love you too, Rion," she said, pulling me into a hug. Her arms wrapped around me like a blanket, and I let myself sink into it. For a moment, I just breathed in.

The silence between us didn't feel so heavy anymore.

Eventually, she pulled back and brushed my hair from my forehead. "Now go get some rest. You look like you're about to fall over."

I laughed, sniffling. "I kind of am."

I stood up, muscles aching, eyes burning. As I walked down the hallway toward my room, I felt... lighter. Not fixed, not fully okay. But the truth was out, and that counted for something.

Still, part of me wondered—what else would I have to let go of next?

But that was a problem for another day.

Chapter 23

Sunday mornings were usually quiet in our house. Slow, peaceful, filled with the smell of fresh coffee and the distant hum of birds outside the window. But not today.

I was barely awake when I heard my mom's voice slicing through the fog of sleep.

"Rion, get up. We're going out to breakfast."

I grunted, pulling the covers tighter around me. "Five more minutes," I mumbled into the pillow, not really processing what she was saying.

"Rion," she called again, firmer this time. "We're going to the country club. Get up."

Country club?

That caught my attention, but only halfway. My mind, groggy and slow, couldn't quite connect the dots yet. I yawned, rubbed the sleep from my eyes, and sat up sluggishly.

The country club? For breakfast? Weird. We never ate there.

Still too tired to think much about it, I grabbed some clothes from the pile on my floor, jeans, a hoodie, and a cap, and shuffled downstairs.

Mom was already at the door, dressed, alert, and holding her keys. She looked way too put-together for a Sunday morning.

"You ready?" she asked, her tone neutral but tight, like she was holding something in.

"Yeah, I guess," I muttered, still rubbing my eyes. "Let's go."

The drive was quiet. Morning light flickered between trees as we passed sleepy houses and shuttered storefronts. I leaned my head against the window, trying to shake off the heaviness in my limbs. My legs were still sore from the day before. My mind ached from everything else, Shawn, Sarah, the job I wasn't supposed to have.

I figured maybe Mom just wanted to talk over pancakes or something. We hadn't really had a proper breakfast together in a while.

But when we pulled into the country club parking lot, everything clicked.

Oh, no.

No. No. No.

This wasn't just a random breakfast outing. This was a setup. My heart thudded hard in my chest. She was taking me here to quit my job. And she hadn't told me, because she knew I wouldn't go willingly.

I sat up straighter, my nerves unraveling as we pulled into a parking space. The beige stucco walls, the neatly trimmed hedges, the navy awnings fluttering in the breeze, everything looked too clean, too calm. My stomach churned.

I scanned the lot, desperate to recognize any familiar cars, hoping no one I worked with was on shift. Sally's beat-up Toyota wasn't here—that was something. A tiny win.

But it didn't mean I was safe.

We walked through the doors, and the familiar scent of brewed coffee and citrus cleaner hit me like a memory. My feet felt heavier with every step.

A hostess I didn't recognize greeted us and led us to a window table near the back of the dining room. I sank into my chair, trying to disappear behind the menu. The morning hum of conversation around us felt too loud, like everyone could hear my heart pounding.

And then I heard the voice I'd hoped to avoid.

"Morning, Miller!"

I looked up to see Sev walking toward us, grinning, his apron still damp. My insides clenched. Just the sight of him made something twist inside me, panic, maybe, or dread. I tried to keep my expression neutral.

"You survived last night's disaster?" Sev asked, loud enough for nearby tables to hear.

I gave him a forced smile, my voice stiff. "Barely."

He slid into the seat beside me like we were just grabbing lunch. "Man, those drunk groomsmen, I swear, I thought Jasmine was gonna kill someone."

I could feel Mom's eyes on me.

"Sev, this is my mom, Allison," I interrupted quickly. "Mom, Sev."

Sev shot her a grin. "Nice to meet you, Mrs. Miller. Rion's told us all about you."

"All good things, I hope," she replied, shaking his hand politely.

"Of course," Sev said. "Your son's a real pro around here, when he's not late, that is." He laughed, and I sank lower in my seat as Mom offered a quiet chuckle.

Sev eventually stood, mentioning something about snagging us the "employee discount" before heading back to the kitchen. I watched him go, wishing the floor would open up and swallow me.

And then I saw him.

Mr. Rickon, the owner of the Country Club, my boss. Towering, tan, intimidating.

He was crossing the dining room, and Mom noticed him too.

Before I could say anything, she was already out of her seat. "Just the person I wanted to see."

"No, no, no—Mom," I hissed under my breath, but she was already walking across the room.

I watched, frozen in horror, as she introduced herself and shook his hand. From the angle, I couldn't hear a word, but I saw it unfold. Mr. Rickon's raised eyebrows, his amused smile, the slow nod. My stomach turned.

A few minutes later, they returned to our table together.

"Rion," Mr. Rickon said warmly, clapping a hand on my shoulder. "Your mom and I had an interesting chat."

Of course you did.

"She filled me in on your situation," he continued. "The whole situation."

I wanted to crawl under the table.

"We've come to a solution," he added. "You'll switch to a seasonal position. Summer's our busiest time anyway—we'd love to keep you on the team."

I blinked. "Wait... seriously? I can stay?"

Mom nodded, her face soft but serious. "Yes. But no more lies. No more hiding."

I felt like the room had tilted sideways. I'd walked in expecting to lose everything. But instead, I was being offered a second chance.

Mr. Rickon patted my back again. "Can't let the club's best tennis player walk away that easily," he said with a wink. "And breakfast is on me today."

He left with a nod, and I stared at the empty space he left behind.

Relief flooded me, but it was tangled up with guilt. I'd lied. Hid everything. And now I was being rewarded with another shot? It didn't seem fair.

I turned to Mom. "I... I don't know what to say."

She reached across the table, squeezed my hand. "You don't have to say anything. I just want you to know I'm proud of you. We'll figure this out together."

My chest ached. Tears stung my eyes, but I blinked them away.

We ate in quiet conversation after that, her voice filling the space between us with stories from her week, little details about work, grocery lists, weekend plans. I nodded along, letting the normalcy settle over me.

And when we stood to leave, I caught sight of Sev again, stepping out of the kitchen with a towel over his shoulder. He spotted me, raised a hand, and smiled.

This time, I smiled back without flinching.

The air outside was crisp as we stepped into the sunlight. I took a deep breath, feeling something loosen in my chest.

"Thank you, Mom," I said, quieter than before.

She smiled and wrapped her arm around my shoulder. "You don't have to thank me, Rion. I've always got your back."

We walked to the car, and for the first time in weeks, I didn't feel like I was bracing for impact. I sat back in the passenger seat, watching the country club disappear behind us as we drove home.

Chapter 24

Another week of school and tennis lessons flew by, and I definitely didn't miss trying to squeeze in shifts at the country club on top of everything else. I couldn't wait for my first real varsity tennis practice.

Since it was still early in the season, official after-school practices wouldn't begin for another week. Coach Konnor had started running three-to-four-hour Saturday morning workouts and team-building practices.

I got to practice early, my breath fogging in the crisp morning air as I dropped my bag and started stretching. The courts were quiet at that hour, the kind of calm I appreciated. It was the last bit of peace before the storm.

Other players started to filter in, and soon, the court buzzed with the shuffle of sneakers on the hard surface and the thwack of tennis balls off rackets. I gripped mine, testing the feel in my hand. The weight was right, the balance perfect—thanks to the new racket Mom had surprised me with a few months back. But something felt off—not with the equipment, but with the atmosphere.

Coach Konnor stood by the fence, arms crossed over his chest, barking instructions as we went through our warm-up drills. It wasn't unusual, he was always tough, but there was something in his tone that rubbed me the wrong way. Sharper than usual. Like he was trying to stay calm while barely holding it together.

"Faster, Miller!" he shouted, eyes narrowing as I sprinted through footwork drills. "Where are your feet today?"

I pushed harder, willing my legs to move faster, but it still wasn't enough.

"Come on! Are you asleep out there?" His voice cut through the air, and I caught a few teammates glancing over. I tried to ignore it and focused on the drill, but the tension stuck like sweat under my shirt.

We moved into hitting drills, and I tried to shake the feeling that something was off. My forehand was solid, backhand crisp, but every time I looked over, Coach Konnor was watching me with an intensity that made my skin crawl.

After a brutal set, I wiped sweat from my brow and glanced at the clock. Practice was almost over, but the unease in my stomach hadn't gone away. He hadn't let up all day. It was starting to feel personal.

"All right, gather around!" he shouted, and we jogged to the net, forming a loose circle around him.

He paced in front of us, hands behind his back, expression tight. "Some of you are looking sharp. Others..." His eyes locked on me a second too long. "...need to get their heads out of the clouds."

My heart sank. He was singling me out. I could feel it.

"Miller, stay behind after practice," he said, not even looking at me as he waved the others off. "I need to have a word with you."

I nodded, feeling every eye on me as the others headed for the locker room. I slung my racket over my shoulder and followed him to the far end of the court, my pulse picking up with every step. I tried to convince myself this was just a routine talk, but I didn't believe it.

"I'm concerned about you, Rion," he started, his voice low and measured, but with an edge that put me on high alert. "I'm not sure where your head's at these days."

I blinked, caught off guard. "My head? I'm focused, Coach. I've been working hard, doing everything I can to—"

He cut me off with a wave of his hand, eyes narrowing. "That's not what I mean." He sighed, rubbing his chin as if he were searching for the right words. "My players can't have any distractions. They need to be focused, dedicated. No drama."

There it was.

My stomach dropped, and it all clicked into place. The way he'd been watching me. The subtle digs during practice. The unease in his tone.

He wasn't talking about my tennis game.

He meant me.

"I don't like 'drama queen' players on my team, Rion," he continued, voice harder now. "It's... distracting to the other players."

I stared at him, heart racing, mind spinning. He didn't say it outright, but I knew exactly what he meant by "drama queen."

He meant gay.

He was using it as a shield, a thin excuse for something deeper. I thought back to the posters, the ones Jason had plastered everywhere, outing me to the school. And I remembered Coach Konnor standing in the hallway that day, watching me tear them down. His face blank. Expression unreadable.

He knew. He'd always known.

"I don't understand, Coach," I said quietly, trying to keep my voice even. "What does any of that have to do with my tennis?"

He didn't answer right away. Just stared, like he was weighing something. Then finally: "Like I said, I don't like distractions. I need players who are fully committed to the team, no outside... issues."

My chest tightened, and I felt a surge of anger rise in my throat. He wasn't even trying to hide it now. He was talking about my sexuality like it was some kind of problem, something that was getting in the way of my game.

But I couldn't blow up. Not here. Not now. If I wanted to stay on this team, I had to keep my cool.

"I am committed, Coach," I said, forcing the words out. "I'm focused. I'm here to win, just like everyone else."

He gave me a tight, forced smile that didn't reach his eyes. "We'll see," he said, his tone dismissive. "We'll see if you're *really* team material."

I stood there, stunned, as he turned and walked away, leaving me alone on the court. My hands trembled as I gripped my racket tighter, my mind reeling from what had just happened.

Did he really just say that? Did a teacher, a coach, basically just tell me that being gay made me a distraction? That my sexuality was somehow a liability to the team?

I didn't even realize I was shaking until I sat down on the bench, my head spinning with anger and disbelief. I stared down at my racket, my fingers numb as I started to put it back in my bag. But when I opened the bag, I froze.

My other racket, my backup, was drenched in pink paint and covered in rainbow glitter.

That was my backup. The one I kept protected for when it mattered most.

For a second, I just stared at it, my brain refusing to process what I was seeing. Then the full weight of it hit me, and a wave of nausea rolled through my stomach.

Someone did this. Someone had gone into my bag and vandalized my racket. Someone thought it would be funny to mock me, again, because of who I was.

The pink paint was still wet, glistening in the sunlight, glitter clinging to the strings like a cruel joke. The message was clear, and it felt personal in a way that made my skin crawl.

I sat there on the court, staring at the ruined racket, the air too still around me. My mind went blank, the world fading into background static. First Mr. Konnor, now this. How was I supposed to keep showing up?

I didn't know how long I sat there, my legs numb and my heart heavy, but eventually, I heard footsteps approaching.

"Hey, Rion, you okay?" one of the guys asked. It was Devon, a junior who usually partnered with me during doubles drills. His voice was hesitant but kind.

I nodded, not trusting myself to speak. I forced a weak smile, gave him a thumbs-up, but inside, I felt like I was crumbling. He and another teammate, Mikey, exchanged uneasy glances. They weren't convinced, but they didn't push. They left me alone, and I was grateful for it.

After a few minutes, I finally packed up my things, carefully placing the ruined racket back in my bag. I didn't even know what to do with it. I couldn't use it, but I couldn't bring myself to throw it away either.

As I started the long walk home, my mind was a whirlwind of emotions—anger, hurt, confusion. I tried to focus on the sound of my sneakers against the pavement, the rhythm of my steps, but it wasn't enough to drown out the storm raging inside me.

For the first time since it all happened, Jason, the posters, and I felt truly alone. Even with Sarah back in my life, even with the friends I'd made along the way, I couldn't shake the feeling that I didn't belong here. Not on this team. Not in this school.

Maybe Mr. Konnor was right. Maybe I was just too much of a "drama queen" to fit in.

But as the thoughts swirled in my mind, I caught a glimpse of something—a tiny spark of defiance, buried deep beneath the hurt and anger.

Chapter 25

The weekend dragged like an endless void, heavy with everything that had happened. I barely left my bed, except to eat or use the bathroom. My mind kept looping back to the moment I pulled out my racket, pink paint, glitter catching the sunlight like a joke I wasn't in on. Every time I closed my eyes, it replayed. Anger. Humiliation. It all bubbled up in my chest, over and over again.

I couldn't tell Mom the truth. She'd been so proud of me, making the tennis team, and holding it all together. If she knew someone was messing with me because of who I was, she'd lose it. So when she knocked on my door asking why I hadn't come out all weekend, I lied.

"Just working on a big school project, Mom," I said, keeping my voice as steady as I could.

She bought it, or pretended to. Either way, she left me alone again. But the silence was starting to get to me. My room felt smaller with every hour. Dim light filtered through the blinds, catching on the clutter of discarded hoodies, snack wrappers, and loose homework pages. My tennis bag sat untouched by the wall, daring me to look inside it again. By Sunday afternoon, the isolation felt like it was choking me. I had to talk to someone.

I grabbed my phone and texted Sarah, the one person who

might actually understand.

Can you come over? Need help with a school project.

Not even a minute later, my phone lit up. Sarah's name flashed on the screen. I hesitated, then picked up.

"School project?" she asked, her voice tinged with confusion. "What are you talking about? We don't have a project due."

I rubbed my temple. "Just come over. I'll explain when you get here."

She paused, and I could almost hear the wheels turning in her head.

"Fine," she said finally. "I'll be there in twenty."

True to her word, twenty minutes later, the front door creaked open. I heard Sarah greeting my mom, saying something about bringing supplies for the project. I smiled, despite everything. She was so quick on her feet, she'd make a great FBI agent one day.

A moment later, my bedroom door opened. Sarah stepped in, balancing a plate of snacks in one hand and a tote bag in the other. She set the plate on my desk and raised an eyebrow.

"Did you bring snacks?" I asked, confused.

She gave me a look, the kind that said *Really, Miller?*

"No, your mom gave me these. Said you probably needed a snack break." She crossed her arms, waiting.

I sighed, the tension still knotted in my shoulders. I reached over the side of my bed, grabbed my tennis bag, and slowly pulled out the racket. The pink paint. The glitter. Even now, it made my stomach twist. My hands hesitated around the frame, like it might burn me. Showing it to someone else felt like exposing a wound.

I turned it so Sarah could see.

Her eyes widened. She froze in place, staring.

There was a beat of silence. The air between us tightened.

She let out a nervous laugh. "Uh... it didn't look like that before, right?"

I glared at her, my face tightening. "No, Sarah, it didn't." My voice wavered. "This is how I found it after practice."

Her smile faded instantly. She sat on the edge of my bed, the mattress sinking slightly under her weight. Her gaze stayed locked on the racket, her jaw tight, like she was still trying to process what she was seeing.

"Who would do this?" she whispered, her voice soft but sharp with anger.

"I don't know," I muttered, pressing my fingers to my temples. "But I have a pretty good guess."

We sat in silence, the weight of it pressing down on both of us. She reached over and squeezed my arm, her grip firm, her expression unreadable for a second, then it softened.

"We'll figure this out, Rion."

Monday came too fast. I barely slept. My mind wouldn't shut up about what might happen. I kept seeing Jason's smug face, the way he taunted me after the posters. I couldn't shake the feeling that he was behind this, too.

Sarah and I walked into school together, trying to act normal. But we were both tense, our eyes scanning the hallways like something might jump out at us. I kept running through options. Tell a teacher? Confront Jason? Do nothing?

Then we turned a corner and saw him. Jason, leaning against a locker, his usual crew around him. My heart kicked up. I was about to look away when he saw me.

"Hey, Miller!" he yelled, loud enough for the whole hallway to turn and stare. "How do you like your new rainbow-bright tennis racket? I think it really brings out your eyes!"

Laughter exploded around him. My face burned. My fists clenched.

Before I even realized it, I was storming toward him.

"Rion!" Sarah grabbed my arm, trying to stop me.

I shook her off.

"What did you just say?" I growled, stopping right in front of him. My voice was low, tight, dangerous.

Jason grinned and leaned in. "You heard me, queer. Fits you."

His friends snickered behind him. My heart pounded, my pulse racing with rage and humiliation.

And then I heard Ashley. Not loud, just muttering, but clear enough.

"Queer."

Sarah snapped. Her eyes flared, and she stepped forward without hesitation.

"Say that again, Ashley, and you and your box-dye disaster of a hairdo are going to regret it."

Ashley blinked, taken off guard. She hadn't expected Sarah to clap back.

But something in me broke, too. I'd had enough of Jason's smirk, the whispers, the locker stares. Enough of pretending it didn't matter.

I shoved Jason. Hard. He stumbled back into the lockers.

The hallway went dead silent.

Jason's grin vanished. "What the hell, Miller?" he snarled, pushing himself off and stepping toward me.

I froze for half a second. My fists clenched.

Then they were flying.

I didn't think. I just hit him. All the anger I'd bottled up, weeks, months, maybe years, poured out in a blur of punches.

My fist connected with his jaw. Pain shot through my knuckles. His fist glanced off my cheek.

Shouts. Footsteps. Chaos.

I didn't hear any of it. I was locked on Jason.

He tried to swing again, but I was faster. I shoved him down, pinned him, and threw another punch.

"Rion, stop!"

Sarah's voice cut through the noise, frantic, far away, but I couldn't stop. Not yet. Not until Jason felt what he'd done.

Then strong arms yanked me back, dragging me off him. I thrashed, trying to break free, but whoever it was held tight. A teacher.

The crowd pulled apart as Mr. Davis, the principal, appeared.

"What the hell is going on here?" he snapped, eyes bouncing between me and Jason was still on the floor, clutching his bloody nose.

Jason smirked, blood on his lip. "Guess Miller can't handle the truth."

"Both of you. My office. Now," Mr. Davis barked. No room for questions.

I didn't fight it. My chest was heaving, my heart still hammering. As I was led away, I glanced back.

Sarah was frozen in the hallway, eyes wide.

The walk to the office was a blur, just noise, footsteps, and heat in my face. My mind kept spinning.

Did I actually just do that? Did I really attack him in front of everyone? *What if I get suspended? What if Mom finds out?*

Chapter 26

I sat on my bed, staring at the wall. The past few days had blurred together, anger, regret, fear, all crashing into a hollow stillness. Now, all that was left was emptiness.

The suspension letter sat on my desk like a scar. Three days, three days away from school, from the team, from everything that made me feel like I belonged somewhere.

I felt crushed. Like I'd fallen off the map and no one had noticed.

My room was dead silent. Too silent. A half-empty water bottle leaned against my nightstand. My backpack slumped near the closet door, still unzipped from Monday. The racket was in the corner, untouched, glinting faintly beneath the overhead light, the glitter still clinging in places.

I kept replaying it all, Jason's face, the moment I snapped, the shock in everyone's eyes. I knew I'd gone too far. But in that moment, the rage had felt unstoppable.

The door creaked. I didn't look up.

Mom.

I heard her footsteps, slow, hesitant—then felt her pause in the middle of the room. She'd been trying to give me space. But I could feel her worry hanging in the air like static.

"Rion," she said softly.

I didn't answer. My throat was locked up, too full of every-thing I didn't know how to say.

The bed dipped as she sat beside me.

"I know you're hurting," she said, her voice barely above a whisper. "And I know I haven't been around as much as I should've been."

That made me glance toward her, just barely.

She looked... tired. Sad. But there was something else in her face, too, something raw. Like she was done pretending things were fine.

"I'm sorry, Rion," she said, her voice cracking. "I know I haven't been the mother you needed me to be. I've been so caught up in my own grief, in my own stuff, I didn't see how much you were hurting. How much you were carrying by yourself."

I sat up a little, my chest tightening. "Mom..."

I didn't even know what I was going to say.

She held up a hand gently. "No, let me finish."

Her voice was quiet, but steady. "I've been thinking a lot about your dad lately. About how, if he were still here, he'd know exactly what to say. He was always better at this kind of thing. He knew how to make you feel like everything was going to be okay, even when it wasn't."

She never talked about him. Ever. Her bringing him up now—especially now, meant more than I could explain.

"I miss him so much," she whispered, eyes glassy. "Every single day. And I know you do too. I should've been there for you more, Rion. I should've helped you through it. But instead, I just... shut down."

My own eyes started to sting. "Mom, you didn't shut down, you were grieving. I get it. I've been trying to be strong for both of us."

She nodded, and her face crumpled. The tears finally came. "I know, sweetheart. And I'm so sorry. You've felt like you had to be the strong one. But you're still just a kid, Rion. You shouldn't have to carry all this alone."

That broke me.

The tears came hard and fast. I reached for her, and she pulled me into her arms, holding me tight. For the first time in forever, I could actually breathe.

"He'd be so proud of you," she whispered into my hair. "Your dad would be proud of the person you've become. Everything you've faced, everything you've done, he'd be proud."

Her words undid me. I sobbed into her shoulder, my body shaking.

It hurt, but at the same time, it felt like something cracked open. Something I'd kept sealed for too long.

As the tears slowed, I pulled back and wiped my face with my sleeve. My cheeks were hot, but my chest felt lighter, like something poisonous had finally been released.

Mom's eyes were red and puffy, but soft. Steady. Safe.

And in that moment, I knew I couldn't keep hiding.

"Mom," I said, my voice trembling. "There's something I need to tell you. Something I've been hiding for a long time."

Her brow creased. "What is it, honey?"

I took a breath. My heart was thudding hard enough to hurt. This was it—the moment I'd spent years circling around, avoiding, burying.

"I'm..." I swallowed. "I'm gay."

The word came out small. Barely louder than a whisper. "I've known for a long time. But I was scared. I didn't know how to tell you. I didn't want you to be disappointed in me."

She didn't even pause. She pulled me into her arms again, tighter than before.

"Oh, Rion," she said, her voice thick with emotion. "I could never be disappointed in you. Not ever."

I let out a breath that shook all the way through me. My whole body trembled. Saying it out loud, it was like dropping a weight I didn't even realize I was still carrying.

"I'm sorry it took me so long," I said, my voice muffled against her shoulder. She pulled back just enough to look me in the eyes, her hands cupping my face gently.

"You don't have to apologize for anything, Rion. I'm so proud of you for telling me. And I'm so sorry you felt like you had to hide this part of yourself from me."

My eyes filled again—but this time, it was pure relief.

For so long, I'd carried this secret like it was something shameful. Terrified of what might happen if it slipped out. But here, with her, I wasn't scared anymore.

"I love you," she said softly, but firmly. "No matter what. I'll always love you."

I smiled through the tears, feeling lighter than I had in years. "I love you too, Mom."

We sat there, holding each other. Breathing together in a steady rhythm.

It was love. Simple. Quiet. And I hadn't realized how much I'd needed it until now.

Eventually, she pulled back, wiping her tears with a shaky laugh. Then she ruffled my hair, smiling the way she used to when I was little and things felt safe.

"You know," she said, her voice gentle, "you didn't have to be afraid to tell me. I've always known there was something special about you, Rion. And this doesn't change that. Not one bit."

Her words settled somewhere deep in me.

Chapter 27

I stepped through the front doors on Thursday morning, heart pounding. Lockers slammed. Voices echoed down the halls. Olympia Heights sounded the same, but it felt different now.

Everyone already knew about the fight. Word spread fast here. I just wasn't sure how they were going to treat me.

I scanned the hall, catching a few glances from other students, some whispering near their lockers. One girl nudged her friend as I passed. I kept my head down.

Then I saw her, Sarah, bouncing on her toes like she'd had too much sugar and not enough patience.

Her face lit up when she spotted me. She rushed over and wrapped me in a dramatic hug.

"Rion!" she cried. "I've been waiting for you! I missed my partner in crime."

I laughed as she pulled back, eyes sparkling. "Yeah, I missed you too."

And I meant it. Seeing her reminded me that no matter how messed up things got, Sarah was still in my corner.

"Oh!" she said suddenly, digging into her bag. "I've been collecting all your missed work. Don't worry, I've got it covered. I even reserved the study room in the library. If we start right after school, you'll be caught up in time for practice this weekend."

She handed me a stack of papers thick enough to bench press.

I groaned. "You are such a bookworm. Honestly, how do you even enjoy this stuff?"

Sarah grinned. "You'll thank me later," she said, winking. "Come on, it's not that bad."

I shook my head, but I couldn't help smiling. She didn't have to do any of this—but she did. And it meant more than I could say.

As we walked down the hallway together, I sighed and glanced at the stack in my hands.

"I can't go to tennis practice this weekend," I said, my voice quieter now. "I got kicked off the team for fighting."

Sarah stopped short. "Wait, what? You got kicked off?"

"Yeah. Zero-tolerance policy. One punch, and I'm out."

Her jaw dropped. "But... Jason wasn't kicked off the baseball team. I saw him yesterday running laps with the rest of them."

I stopped too. My stomach twisted.

"Of course he wasn't," I muttered. "Jason gets special treatment. Always has."

Her eyes narrowed. "That is complete bullshit. How does he get away with everything?"

I shrugged. "That's just how it is. No point in fighting it."

But she didn't back down. If anything, she looked like she was ready to go to war.

"Oh, no," she said, her voice low. "This isn't over. If Jason stays, so do you. I'm not letting this slide."

I raised an eyebrow. "What are you going to do?"

She grinned. "Just trust me."

And somehow, that was both comforting and terrifying.

By the time the final bell rang, I was more drained than I

expected. Catching up on missed work and dodging sideways stares all day had worn me out.

But then I saw Sarah near the library, arms crossed, fire in her eyes. She didn't even give me time to ask.

"Come on," she said, already pulling me down the hall. "We've got a meeting to attend."

My stomach flipped as we rounded a corner—and saw the principal's office.

"Sarah," I hissed. "What are you doing?"

She didn't even blink.

Inside, Principal Davis and Coach Konnor sat waiting. Davis looked mildly confused. Konnor didn't look up.

"Principal Davis, Mr. Konnor," Sarah began, voice steady, "thank you for meeting with us."

Davis folded his hands. "What's this about, Miss Russell?"

She squared her shoulders, calm and fierce. "This is about Rion being unfairly removed from the tennis team. If he's out for fighting, then Jason Banks should be off the baseball team too."

Konnor leaned forward, his face pinching with irritation. "Miss Russell, we have policies in place for a reason. Rion broke them. There are consequences."

"I'm aware," Sarah said. "But Rion was provoked. Jason Banks has been bullying him for months. That's a violation of your zero-bullying policy."

Principal Davis's brow furrowed. "Miss Russell."

"I'm not done," Sarah snapped. She pulled a folder from her bag and laid it on the desk. "These are statements from students who witnessed Jason's bullying. They're willing to go on record."

I blinked. How did she even get those?

Davis flipped through the pages. His frown deepened.

"And," Sarah continued, "I also have a list of faculty who reported Jason's behavior, only to be told to ignore it."

Principal Davis's face flushed. "That's not true," he said sharply. "We take all reports seriously."

Sarah's eyes narrowed. "Do you? Because it seems like some students are protected while others are punished. And speaking of unfair treatment..." She turned to Mr. Konnor. "I've got students who heard you call Rion a 'drama queen.'"

My chest tightened.

Konnor stiffened. Sweat glistened at his temples. "I don't know what you're talking about."

"Oh, don't worry," Sarah said, cool as ice. "I've got names. And they're willing to talk. I'm sure the local press would love to hear about a coach making homophobic remarks to a student athlete."

Principal Davis leaned back, silent for a long moment.

Finally, he spoke: "Miss Russell, that's a serious accusation."

"I know," Sarah said calmly. "And I'm prepared to go public with it."

The silence in the room was brutal. You could hear the clock ticking.

Then Davis turned to me. "Rion, you're reinstated to the tennis team. Effective immediately."

I sat there, stunned. Did that really just happen?

"Wait, what?" I asked.

Sarah beamed. "Thank you, Principal Davis. I knew you'd make the right choice."

Coach Konnor said nothing. His face was red, jaw clenched tight. He didn't look at me.

But I looked at him.

I stood up and followed Sarah into the hallway. The door clicked shut behind us.

"That was... insane," I said, still trying to process everything.

Sarah grinned. "What can I say? I've been watching a lot of Law & Order."

I laughed, the tension breaking like a popped balloon. "That was peak Miranda Hobbes."

"Obviously."

We walked side by side down the corridor, the weight on my shoulders starting to lift. I didn't know how she pulled it off, but she did. I was back. And maybe, finally, Jason would face the consequences he deserved.

"I think I want to be a lawyer now," Sarah said, half-joking.

"You'd kill it."

We pushed through the front doors into the afternoon sun. It spilled across the pavement in gold streaks, warm on my face.

Chapter 28

The weeks had flown by in a blur of tennis matches, schoolwork, and the constant buzz of adrenaline as our varsity team tore through the season. Every match so far had felt like a warm-up, almost boring. I played second seed singles for our team and hadn't lost a match all season.

Not only did I qualify for Singles Sectionals, but I made it to the Semifinals, and I was one win away from something huge. My confidence was sky-high.

But that day was different.

From the second I stepped onto the court, something felt off. My grip was too tight. The air felt heavier. My legs, a little slower. I tried to brush it off, probably nerves. This was the biggest match of the season, after all.

The crowd buzzed. Bleachers packed with students, parents, and teachers. I spotted Sarah waving, her red hair a beacon in the stands. Right beside her, like always, was Shawn. He hadn't missed a single match. He hadn't spoken to me either. Just sat there, watching. Then he disappeared before I could say a word.

That distance still stung, no matter how much I tried to pretend it didn't.

My opponent was someone I didn't recognize. Scrappy, with a chipped front tooth and a racket that looked like it had survived a war. Not polished like most of the players I'd faced. But his eyes, sharp and focused, sent a ripple of unease through me.

The match started, and from the first rally, I was scrambling. He was everywhere. No matter how hard I hit or where I placed the ball, he hunted it down like a dog with something to prove. His style was messy, unpredictable, but relentless.

Before I could blink, the first set was over.

2–6.

I slumped onto the bench, sweat clinging to my temples as I tried to catch my breath. My chest felt tight, like my lungs were shrinking by the second. All season, I'd been steady. Focused. And now I was unraveling in front of a crowd that felt more like an audience waiting for me to fall.

What the hell was happening?

I ran my hands through my hair, eyes locked on the court, hoping it would offer some kind of answer. But it didn't. My thoughts twisted around each other, looping too fast to grab hold of.

I have to win.

I have to get to—

No. Don't think about that. Just focus. One point at a time.

But my heartbeat thudded against my ribs like a warning I couldn't ignore. Had I let everything, Shawn, the suspension, the stress, get inside my head? I could feel it all pressing against me, like the air had thickened.

I stood abruptly and signaled the chair ump for a bathroom break. When the whistle blew, I didn't hesitate. I needed space. Distance. A second to breathe.

The hallway lights buzzed overhead, casting a sterile glow. My sneakers squeaked against the linoleum as I moved fast, not thinking, just moving—until I shoved open the bathroom door and crashed into someone.

I caught myself against the frame, muttering an automatic, "Sorry," before even looking up.

Then I did.

And froze.

It was Shawn.

His eyes widened a little, but he smiled—just a little. "You still haven't learned to watch where you're going, Miller," he said, teasing. His voice was lighter than I expected, like some of the tension had softened since the last time we spoke.

Before I could say anything, another voice cracked through the hallway.

"Miller!"

Coach Konnor's voice was sharp and impatient, his footsteps heavy as he approached. His gaze ping-ponged between the two of us, confusion knitting across his face.

"What the hell are you doing? You've got five minutes for a bathroom break. This isn't a damn social hour."

Shawn jumped in before I could even open my mouth. "We just bumped into each other, Coach. Literally."

Coach didn't look convinced. "Bumped into each other, huh?" He let out a bitter little laugh, then shook his head. "Yeah, well, get back on the court. You've got a match to lose."

The jab landed hard. I clenched my jaw, staying quiet, watching him walk off down the hallway like he'd already decided the outcome.

I turned back to Shawn, pulse still racing but for an entirely different reason now. "Sorry," I blurted. "I didn't mean to make things weird. I just..."

He took a small step closer. "Rion," he said quietly, "you didn't misread anything."

I blinked. My heart skipped.

"I'm just not ready," he added. "Not yet."

Before I could say a word, he leaned in and kissed me—just a soft press of lips to cheek, barely more than a moment, but enough to short-circuit my thoughts.

When he pulled back, his expression was calm. Kind. "Good luck coming back from a set down."

Then he turned and walked away, like he hadn't just turned my insides to fire.

I stood frozen in place, my hand drifting to my cheek, still tingling.

He hadn't pushed me away. He hadn't pretended that nothing happened. He was just figuring it out—same as me. And maybe, for now, that was enough.

I exhaled, steadied myself, and headed back to the court.

Coach Konnor watched me return with arms crossed and a sour expression, but I barely registered it. My thoughts were still full of Shawn's words, his voice, the way he hadn't looked afraid.

I grabbed my racket and took my place on the baseline, grounding myself with each bounce of the ball. The sun had shifted across the court, slicing it into sharp angles of light and shadow. I focused on the feel of the grip in my hand, the weight of the moment.

Chapter 29

The weight of the first-set loss sat heavily on my shoulders. Shawn's kiss, Konnor's snide comment, the pressure of the semis, it all crackled in my head like static. I shook it off. Pushed it down. Focused.

Bounce. Bounce. I gripped the ball, trying to steady my nerves. The crowd murmured behind me, a low hum.

None of it mattered. Just the next point.

Across the net, my opponent bounced on his toes. Scrappy. Restless. The kind of player who turned every rally into a war of attrition. He'd been chasing down everything since the first serve, and I was still reeling.

Love all. My serve.

I took a breath, tossed the ball, swung.

The ball clipped the net. Dropped back on my side.

"Fault."

I stepped back and exhaled. "Focus, Rion."

I tossed. My mind spun. My arm felt stiff. The second serve floated, *too soft.*

He pounced, drove it deep into the corner. I reached it late, barely scraping a return over the net.

He crushed the next forehand past me.

"Love–fifteen."

I clenched my jaw. My grip tightened around the handle. This couldn't be slipping away, not now.

Bounce. Bounce. The crowd quieted.

Then...

"You've got this, Miller!"

Shawn's voice, clear, strong, cut through the noise like sunlight breaking through clouds.

I glanced up. There he was, standing in the bleachers, clapping. His smile was real. Proud.

My heart kicked. And then...

"Let's go, Rion!" Sarah's voice rang out next.

One by one, others joined in—clapping, cheering, calling my name.

The air shifted. Energy surged through me. They weren't just watching anymore. They were behind me.

I stepped to the line. Deep breath. Toss. Swing.

The serve blasted down the T. He didn't even move.

"Fifteen—all."

I wiped the sweat from my brow. A fresh pulse of confidence shot through me.

Bounce. Toss. Crack, another serve down the line.

He reached it, barely.

I stepped in and ripped a forehand cross court. Clean winner.

"Thirty—fifteen."

The crowd roared.

I stepped up again. Grip solid. Mind sharp.

Served wide, pulled him out. His return floated high.

I raced in. Hammered a backhand down the line. He didn't even twitch.

"Forty—fifteen."

Tossed high. Swung full force. The ball screamed down the

middle, ace. The bleachers exploded.

"Game, Miller. One−love."

I exhaled. Only then did I realize I'd been holding my breath.

The momentum had flipped.

I grabbed my towel and wiped my face, mind flashing through the last few points. That shift, that crack in his armor, I saw it now.

He hated flat shots.

I'd noticed it in the second set—the way he flinched when the ball came at him fast and low, the stutter in his swing, the slight panic behind his eyes. He preferred topspin, slow rallies, and looping balls he could track and reset. But flat shots? Those came in fast, no arc, little margin for error. They were high-risk, high-reward. Harder to control. But brutal when executed right.

Which meant they were perfect for this.

No more playing it safe.

Across the net, he stepped up to serve, trying to shake off the last game. I watched his shoulders rise and fall. He bounced the ball three times, like always. A little ritual to reset.

But I could feel it.

The shift. The tilt of the match. It buzzed beneath my skin, coiling through my limbs like a live wire.

My hands trembled, but not from fear. My heart pounded like a drum. My breath came shallow. Legs tight. Every muscle is on alert.

The crowd blurred into silence.

Just the court. The ball. He and me.

I'm locked in.

When it was my serve, I didn't hold back. I ripped flat shots down the line and into the corners. Fast. Aggressive. No topspin to slow the bounce—just pure speed. My racket became a weapon. Each point built on the last. Aces, clean winners, forehand missiles he couldn't chase down.

He couldn't adjust.

His timing faltered, his footwork got sloppy, and soon he was bleeding unforced errors, shots soaring long, volleys into the net, frustrated groans between points.

I had him.

And I wasn't letting up.

I pushed through the last game with fire in my veins. One last serve, flat and fast, skidded off the baseline. He swung too late. Frame hit. The ball sailed.

Wide.

The umpire's voice rang clear, slicing through the noise.

"Game, set, match, Miller. Two sets to one. 6−2, 4−6, 3−6."

For a split second, the world stilled.

Then it exploded.

My teammates burst onto the court, a rush of cheers, arms, and back slaps. Laughter and shouts filled the air, but one voice rose above the rest, "You're going to the finals!" It echoed like a firework in my chest, bright and exploding.

Chapter 30

The sun was barely up, casting a soft orange glow across the neighborhood as I pulled myself out of bed. My alarm clock blinked 6:00 a.m., and even in my groggy state, adrenaline had already started to kick in. Today was the day, the sectional finals. The biggest match of my life.

My heart fluttered with a mix of excitement and nerves as I got dressed, pulling on my tennis gear and trying to quiet the pressure building in my chest.

My phone buzzed.

Greg: *Let's go, Miller. We both know you need hitting practice before the finals.*

No time to second-guess myself. I grabbed my tennis bag and headed down the hallway. I needed to loosen up before the match, shake off the jitters.

When I reached the kitchen, Mom was already up, nursing her coffee at the counter.

"Morning," she said with a soft smile. "Ready for the big day?"

I nodded, though it probably came off more like a shrug. "Yeah. Just heading to get some practice in with Greg."

She watched me for a second, her expression warm and steady. "You're going to do great, Rion. No matter what happens out there, I'm proud of you."

I gave her a small smile, grabbed a granola bar from the counter, and slipped out the door.

The school tennis courts were empty when I arrived, except for Greg bouncing a ball against the pavement. The soft thuds echoed in the quiet morning air. Just the two of us.

"Hey, man," Greg called, giving me a nod. "You ready for this?"

"Yeah, I think so." I tried to keep my voice even, even as nerves twisted in my stomach. "Could use a few good rallies to settle in."

Greg grinned, that easy confidence of his was always kind of contagious. He tossed me a ball. "Let's do it."

We started hitting, just warm-up stuff. Easy rallies, nothing fancy. The steady rhythm—the thwack of the ball, the shuffle of our feet—grounded me. For a while it was just movement and muscle memory: back and forth, hit and recover.

The tension in my shoulders started to ease. My shots landed clean. I wasn't overthinking anymore. I was just playing.

Then I went for a hard, flat forehand to the corner.

PING.

I froze.

The ball sailed long, but I barely noticed. I looked down at my racket, one of the strings had snapped, curling loose like a broken nerve.

"You've gotta be kidding me," I muttered, staring at it like it had betrayed me on purpose.

Greg jogged over. "Did your string just break?"

I nodded. "Yeah. Perfect timing, right?"

He glanced at my bag. "You've got a backup, though, right?"

I hesitated.

My stomach dropped.

Technically... yeah. I had a backup.

I walked over and pulled it out. The racket Jason had vandalized, still streaked with dried pink paint and flecks of glitter.

I held it up. "You mean my 'pretty pretty princess' racket?"

Greg stared at it for a second before bursting out laughing. "It's... definitely something..."

I laughed too, even though it still stung to look at it. But laughing helped. It shook off the frustration, making the moment feel less like a disaster.

Greg wiped a tear from his eye. "Man. I've gotta say—I haven't exactly been the greatest team captain this year. With all the crap that went down with Jason... and Coach treating you like garbage... I should've had your back more."

I shrugged. "We all had stuff to deal with. You've still been here."

He paused. "Still, maybe next year you should be captain."

I looked at him like he'd lost his mind. "Me? Captain? I can barely keep myself together. I just want to play. Not lead."

Greg shook his head. "You've been leading all year, you just didn't realize it. You stood up to Jason. You stood up to Coach. You never quit. That's what a captain looks like."

I didn't know what to say. I just stared down at the glitter-covered racket in my hand and tried, really tried, to picture myself as captain.

Greg grinned. "Hey, we're all figuring it out. But you've come a long way. The whole team has. It's like we're a family now, even if everyone hates Coach Konnors."

I burst out laughing. Greg joined in.

It was the first time all morning I felt genuinely relaxed. Like the weight of the day had lifted, even if just for a second.

Greg raised an eyebrow, nodding toward the racket. "Team captain stuff aside, what are you going to do? Actually play with that thing?"

I sighed, running my hand down the grip. "Yeah. It's all I've got."

He smirked. "You're really going to walk into the finals with glitter flying off your racket?"

I looked at it again, still ridiculous. Still covered in pink streaks and sparkles. But something about it felt right.

"Yeah," I said. "It's kind of a statement."

Greg squinted. "A statement?"

I nodded, gripping it tighter. "Look at it. It's a mess. But it's *my* mess. It's everything I've been through this season. And I'm still here. Still playing. That means something."

I wrapped the handle with a fresh layer of white grip tape and we stepped back onto the court.

Greg smirked as we resumed rallying. "Just a heads-up. Glitter keeps flying off every time you swing. You're basically playing in a rainbow cloud."

I glanced down at the racket and laughed, shaking my head. I probably looked ridiculous.

But somehow, I felt powerful.

"I guess if I'm gonna play," I said, grinning, "I might as well do it in style."

Chapter 31

The Sectional Finals were at 10 a.m., and getting in an early hit with Greg had taken just enough of the edge off to keep me steady. This was it. I was facing Mathew Davis, the top seed. Everything I'd worked for all season came down to this one match.

I dressed slowly, tugging on my team uniform like armor. My hands shook, trembled. My muscles were wound tight, like a string pulled taut and ready to snap.

In the kitchen, Mom sat sipping her second coffee, calm in a way I couldn't fathom.

"You ready to head out?" she asked, looking up with that quiet steadiness she always seemed to have when I needed it most.

"I think so," I said, voice thinner than I wanted. I nodded anyway, hoping courage would show up somewhere between the driveway and the court.

The drive to the finals was quiet.

Not awkward, just tense. My mom sipped her coffee, eyes focused on the road. I stared out the window, watching the town slip by in a blur. Each block felt heavier than the last.

We turned off the main road and into a nicer part of town. Big houses. Neatly trimmed lawns. Definitely not where I was from.

Then the school came into view. Eastside Prep.

It looked like a college campus. Huge brick buildings, clean tennis courts with tall fences, and real bleachers. Everything about it looked sharp. Intimidating. Like the kind of place that is expected to win.

The air buzzed with nervous energy, like the whole place was holding its breath.

I stepped out of the car and slung my tennis bag over my shoulder.

Mom gave my arm a squeeze. "You okay?"

I nodded, even though my stomach was doing flips. "Yeah."

Whether I was or not, it didn't matter.

It was game day.

I grabbed my bag from the car and headed toward the courts. My legs dragged, not with fatigue, but like the ground was made of wet cement.

The parking lot was already packed. Team vans lined the far end, school logos painted across the windows. Players stretched near the courts. Coaches gave last-minute advice. Parents hovered with coffees and folding chairs, chatting in low, nervous tones.

A handful of doubles matches were already underway, but I barely glanced at them. I had my own match to worry about, no distractions, not today.

Coach Konnors and my teammates were already gathered by the bench. For once, Coach didn't have that usual bulldog scowl. His arms were crossed, but his expression was almost... neutral.

He looked me over for a second, then cleared his throat.

"Miller," he said. "Just play like you've been playing. Don't overthink it. It's just tennis."

Just tennis?

I glanced around. A few teammates exchanged looks, eyebrows raised, lips twitching like they wanted to laugh but knew better. We were all thinking the same thing, but no one said it.

I gave Coach a small nod and forced a half-smile. But my brain was already somewhere else, locked on the court, the crowd, and the six-foot-tall obstacle waiting for me at the net.

Mathew Davis stood court side, arms loose at his sides, expression unreadable. We were supposed to walk out together, but neither of us said a word. The chair umpire stepped between us and flicked a coin into the air.

"Davis, call it."

"Heads."

The coin landed. The umpire nodded and took his seat.

"Welcome to the Sectional Finals. Best of three sets. To the left, Rion Miller. To the right, Mathew Davis. Davis won the toss and will serve first. Five-minute warm-up starts now."

I stepped onto the court and took a deep breath, letting it fill every tense corner of my body. *Focus. Find rhythm. Don't look ahead, just play.*

No glitter flew off my racket this time. The grip felt solid. Clean.

Maybe that meant something. Maybe I'd finally shaken off everything that had weighed me down this season.

Mathew warmed up like a machine—sharp footwork, fluid strokes, zero wasted motion. He didn't just move across the court; he owned it. Every shot carried the quiet confidence of someone who had done this a thousand times before. This wasn't a friendly match to him. He came here to win.

"Players have one minute before play begins," the umpire called out.

I returned to the bench and toweled off, trying to calm my breath. My heart was hammering, but I kept my face steady.

Then I looked up and froze.

There they were.

My mom. The entire Russell family. Sarah and Shawn, front and center. All of them wearing matching shirts that read MILLER IS #1 in huge, bold letters.

A rush of emotion surged through me, sharp and sudden. I hadn't expected them. I hadn't asked. But they came.

Then I saw them, scattered across the other side of the bleachers: Sally, Sev, Chen, Grace, Luke, all my friends from the country club. Cheering. Smiling. Waving like they'd been waiting for this all season.

The noise of the crowd dimmed under the weight of that realization. I wasn't out here alone.

Their presence didn't just lift me, it braced me. Grounded me. Like reinforcements arriving in the final battle.

This match wasn't just about a trophy or a title.

It was about everything it took to get here.

Everyone who stood beside me.

I swallowed hard, blinking back the rising burn behind my eyes. My grip tightened around the racket. My spine straightened. My heartbeat didn't slow, but now it had purpose.

The umpire's voice crackled back into the air.

"Time. Players, ready."

I walked to the baseline and planted my feet. My fingers adjusted the grip one last time. I could hear the crowd settling behind me, but I blocked it all out.

Just the ball. Just the court.

You've trained for this. You've fought for this.

Trust it.

I exhaled slowly.
Then I looked across the net and nodded.

Chapter 32

The crowd buzzed, tension spiking as I stepped onto the court. The warm-up felt more like a preview of the war ahead than a formality.

Mathew stood across from me, calm, focused, already locked in. His strokes were sharp and deliberate. Every rally landed with weight. He wasn't holding back. But what rattled me most was his control, like he saw the court three moves ahead.

Even in warm-up, the guy was terrifying.

I took a deep breath and glanced up into the stands.

There was Mom with the Russells. Sarah and Shawn are still front and center, rocking *MILLER IS #1* shirts.

And then my crew from the country club, Sally, Sev, Chen, Grace, Luke, all waving like maniacs. For a moment, the nerves lightened.

I tightened my grip on the racket. Time to go.

Mathew came out swinging.

His serve exploded off the court, clean, brutal. He held his first game without dropping a point. I scrambled just to stay in rallies. He was dictating every exchange, using angles, spinning me wide, then crushing shots down the line.

My first service game was steadier, but I was behind. Always behind.

His rallies felt like chess matches, and I was losing the board.

I chased, stretched, burned. My legs screamed. My lungs fought for air.

Suddenly it was 4-all, and I was serving at 30–40. Break point.

I bounced the ball, trying to steady my hands. My heart rattled in my chest. I needed something, anything to shift this.

I tossed it high. Swung hard. Fastest serve of my life.

Mathew was already there, blasting a cross-court winner like he knew it was coming.

He dominated my last service game. It wasn't just that he broke my serve—he dismantled it. Every return came back harder, faster, like my shots barely mattered. Losing a service game was always rough, but this break felt like a punch to the gut.

Now he was serving at 5–4 for the set.

I trudged to the baseline, shoulders sagging, jaw clenched. I couldn't look at anyone in the stands. Their expectations pressed in like a weight I couldn't dodge.

Then—

"Come on, Rion!"

"You've got this!"

"Focus, Rion!"

Mom's voice. Sarah's. The roar behind them building. Laughing. Believing.

Their energy lit something in me. I straightened. Just enough to feel steady.

Mathew stepped up to serve, cool and dangerous.

We rallied hard. At 40–30, he hit an ace down the T.

A clean Line kiss. Set, 6–4.

I exhaled slowly. No panic. I'd been here before.

Walking to my chair, I felt every inch of strain. I dropped into my seat and pulled the towel over my head.

Reset. Refocus.

My brain spun, but I latched onto one thought: *This isn't over. I've come back from worse.*

I drew in a deep breath and let it out slowly, grounding myself. The umpire called time. I rolled my shoulders, shook out my arms, and stood. This match wasn't over.

The second set turned into a slugfest. We traded service games and breaks, locked in rallies that stretched for what felt like forever. The score was tied, but this time, I refused to back off.

At 30–all, I carved a wide slice that pulled Mathew off balance. He lunged, barely catching it. The return floated, slow and high. I stepped in, locked on, and crushed it with an overhead smash. The crowd erupted.

"40–30, Miller," the umpire called.

The surge of confidence hit hard. I bounced into my next serve—clipped the net, fault. I didn't flinch. Second serve: high kick to the deep corner. Mathew lunged, misfired into the net.

"Game, Miller." 5–4.

For the first time all match, I wasn't chasing, I was leading.

Mathew stepped up to serve, but something in him had shifted. His first serve went long. The second? Into the net. Double fault. His jaw tightened. I stayed locked in, focused. Four unforced errors later, I had the game.

"Set, Miller. Six games to four," the umpire called.

The crowd roared, the sound bouncing off every surface like a tidal wave. I walked to my bench, chest heaving, soaked in sweat, but buzzing with belief. Momentum had finally tilted my way.

Mathew looked drained. But I was, too.

Time.

I opened the final set with a shaky service game, and it cost me. My nerves got the better of me—tight, rushed, overeager. I lost it.

But Mathew gave it right back. Another double fault. 1–1.

We clawed through the next few games, trading holds, breaking each other back.

3–3.

I broke him with a clean forehand down the line and barely held my next serve. 4–3.

Every muscle screamed. My shirt clung to me, sweat soaking every inch. But I didn't stop. Couldn't.

Then, Mathew unraveled.

His next service game opened with two straight double faults. When his return floated high on the third point, instinct took over. I hammered it at his feet. He stumbled. Missed.

"Love–40," the umpire said.

One point away from serving for the match.

My heart pounded in my throat. Mathew tossed the ball, and slammed it straight into the net.

Another double fault.

Stunned, I froze, staring at the umpire.

He'd cracked.

"Game, Miller."

The crowd exploded. My teammates were on their feet, chanting. "Miller! Miller!"

The roar was deafening.

5–3. My serve. This was it.

The moment I'd bled for. Fought for. Everything had led to

166

this. My hands trembled as I bounced the ball. Narrowed my focus.

First serve, wide and deep. Mathew lunged, flicked it cross-court.

I stepped in and crushed a flat forehand down the line.

Winner.

"15–love," the umpire called.

The crowd erupted again.

I turned toward the baseline, fist pumping, heart racing.

So close, I could taste it.

Chapter 33

I looked to the stands, Mom, Sarah, Shawn, all on their feet, clapping and cheering, their eyes locked on mine, willing me forward. For a second, everything else fell away. It was just me, the court, and the game.

Mathew stood across from me, calm and ready. Focused. Loose. He'd been solid all match, but I could finish this.

I tossed the ball high, my racket snapping forward as I sent the serve deep. Mathew returned it clean, and the rally was on, this could be it. We hammered groundstrokes back and forth, neither of us backing down. My legs burned, lungs tight, but I stayed with him. I ripped a flat shot cross-court, low and fast. Looked clean. Mathew wasn't even close to it.

And yet somehow he got there. Instinct and speed.

He slid into the shot and flicked a soft, spinning drop shot that kissed the net and rolled just over. Impossible.

I sprinted, feet pounding, heart thudding. I slid, stretched, barely scraped under the ball and flicked it back.

It dropped. Once. Twice.

Point, mine.

The crowd erupted, but the noise barely registered.

Because the pain came fast. Blinding.

Something tore through my ankle like fire. My leg buckled. I collapsed hard, grabbing at my foot as the world tilted sideways. The cheering turned to static. My ears rang.

No. No, no, no.

"Rion!"

Voices, distant and warped, like underwater.

Mathew sprinted over, clearing the net in one leap. He dropped to his knees beside me, eyes wide. "Rion, are you okay?"

I couldn't answer. Couldn't speak. My throat locked as the pain pulsed in sharp, dizzying waves.

Mathew turned, waving to the sideline, yelling for help. Seconds later, Coach Konnor and my mom rushed over, panic all over their faces.

My vision blurred. I blinked fast, trying to keep the tears at bay. Not now. Not like this.

They helped me sit up, barely. I couldn't put weight on it. With Coach on one side and Mathew on the other, they lifted me to my feet. Each step was agony, but the silence was worse. The entire crowd held its breath.

"Let me take a look," Coach said, kneeling beside me. He pressed gently around the joint, and I clenched my jaw with every touch. His brow furrowed before he let out a sigh. "It feels like a rolled ankle, Rion."

The words hit like a punch to the gut. I looked away, blinking fast. This couldn't be it.

Mom crouched next to me, her hand on my shoulder. "Rion, it's okay. You don't have to keep going. We'll get it checked out."

Her voice was soft. Too soft. It made everything worse.

"I'm not done," I said, my voice shaking. I looked at Coach. "Just tape it."

He opened his mouth to argue, but the look on my face stopped him. He sighed and reached for the tape.

Mom looked bewildered, then leaned in. "Rion, you don't have to keep playing."

"Yes, I do," I said in one quick breath. "Coach, tape it up."

She looked at Coach Konnor, her nod hesitant, worry written all over her face.

The crowd stayed quiet, watching every move as Coach wrapped the ankle. Pressure closed in around my chest, heavy and tight. Could I really keep going? Doubt flared. I shoved it down.

I had to finish.

Mathew stood nearby, unreadable. Even he looked stunned. Coach tied off the wrap, eyes filled with concern.

"You sure about this, Miller?"

I nodded. "Yeah."

No turning back now.

I limped toward the baseline, testing my footing. Every step was a warning, pain shooting up my leg. Mathew watched me, part respect, part worry. The whole court stood still, the match hanging in the air.

The score: 30–all.

I bounced the ball, fingers trembling. My ankle throbbed. My vision swam.

First serve, wild. Way off.

A gasp rippled through the stands.

I reset, tossed the ball again.

Second serve, soft, no power, no spin.

Mathew stepped in and crushed the return past me. No chance.

"30–40," the umpire said.

Tears stung my eyes. My body screamed.

One more try.

I served with a little more pace, but Mathew was ready. His return came deep. I pushed off to chase it, and my ankle gave away under me.

I stumbled, barely catching myself. The pain exploded.

I froze. Tears streamed down my face.

I couldn't do this. Couldn't move. Couldn't fight. The pain was bad, but the disappointment cut deeper.

I looked across the net and shook my head.

Mathew saw it. He didn't say a word. His expression softened.

Just like that, the match ended.

I limped to the net, racket dangling from my fingers. I looked at the chair umpire. "I'm retiring."

The words were jagged glass in my throat.

"Miller is retiring," the umpire called. "Game, set, match, Davis."

It was over.

Mathew stepped forward, offered his hand. I took it. He pulled me into a hug.

"You know this was your title, right?" he said.

I smiled through the blur. "No, Mathew. It's yours. But I'll take it next year."

He laughed. "Oh yeah? Better heal up fast. Let's swap numbers. I could use a hitting partner before I head to college."

I wiped my face. "You just need someone to keep you humble, huh?"

"Exactly," he grinned.

The loss still sat heavy in my chest, but something in his words lit a spark. This wasn't the end.

The crowd erupted again, not just for the winner, but for the match. For the fight. For both of us.

As I limped off the court, Mom on one side and Coach on the other, a storm of emotion swirled inside me. Yeah, I lost.

But not really.

I looked back once. The crowd was still cheering. The court glowed under the late morning sun, the lines, the net, the place where I'd left everything I had.

There'd be other matches. Other finals.

And I'd be ready.

Chapter 34

After the match, my ankle throbbed with every heartbeat. I tried to ignore it, but hiding it was getting harder by the minute.

Mom didn't give me a chance to argue. She drove us straight to the ER. I didn't protest. Between the crash of adrenaline and the sting of retiring, I felt numb. The swelling had already started, a dark bruise forming along the side of my ankle. I told myself it wasn't that bad, but a quiet disappointment sat heavy in my chest.

On the ride to the hospital, the last moments of the match kept looping in my head, Mathew's voice, the handshake, the hug. It didn't feel real yet. I'd been so close. And even though I was proud, some stubborn part of me kept whispering, *What if you hadn't rolled your ankle?*

The ER visit was quick. X-rays confirmed no break, just a bad sprain. Ice. Rest. Elevation.

Mom exhaled, "It could've been so much worse." I nodded. "Yeah. I'm already feeling better." We shared tired smiles as we left the hospital.

I figured we'd head home. Instead, we pulled into the Russells driveway. The lights were on. Music drifted from the backyard. Laughter echoed around the fence.

"Everyone's here to celebrate you," Mom said as we walked

to the side gate. "Finals or not, you earned it."

As we stepped into the yard, a wave of cheers hit me. My teammates, coworkers from the club, the Russells, everyone was there. Pizza boxes stacked high. Soda cans littered the table. Kids splashed in the pool. Music thumped from a Bluetooth speaker.

Sarah rushed over and wrapped her arms around me, nearly knocking me over.

"You were amazing!" she squealed. "I was stressed the whole time. I don't know how you stayed calm!"

I leaned on my good leg, laughing. "I didn't." I winced as I shifted my weight. "I was panicking the entire time. You know, classic Rion."

Greg, team captain and unofficial king of post-match pizza, raised his slice in salute.

"You played like a beast, Rion. That win was yours, man."

I shook my head, smiling. "I tried. There's always next year."

By the pool, Sally waved me over. "Rion! Get over here. We've been analyzing every rally. Your serve? Meh. Your footwork? Beautiful. We'll fix the rest this summer."

I limped over. "Yeah, right after I stop walking like a baby giraffe."

Sev grinned. "Dude, the glitter racket? Legendary."

I laughed. "Hey, it definitely made a statement. Maybe I'll start a trend."

Everyone cracked up. For a while, all the stress melted away. We rehashed the match, joked about Coach Konnor's terrible pep talks, and debated whether my third-set drop shot was genius or just dumb luck.

I was mid-bite into a slice of pepperoni when I noticed Shawn weaving through the crowd. He'd been quiet all evening, hanging back by the pool, but now he was headed straight toward me.

My chest tightened.

"Rion," he said, stopping beside my chair. "Can we talk? Just us?" I wiped my hands on a napkin and stood, still a little shaky on my feet.

"Sure," I said, a little too quickly.

We slipped inside, away from the music and laughter. My heart pounded as I followed him into the kitchen, nerves prickling down my spine. The room was dim and still, the hum of the refrigerator the only sound.

Shawn turned to face me. His eyes were steady, his voice soft.

"I just wanted to say... congratulations. You were incredible out there. And I know you'll be back in the finals next year.

His words landed gently, but there was something else underneath. Something heavier.

"Thanks," I said, leaning back against the counter.

Shawn rubbed the back of his neck. "I need to talk about that night. When you kissed me."

My breath hitched. It was the first time we'd acknowledged it since it happened. The emotions I'd shoved down started bubbling to the surface.

"Shawn, you don't have to—"

"No. Let me finish." He held up a hand. "I was confused, Rion. I didn't know how to react. I've been... questioning a lot. About myself. And when you kissed me, it caught me off guard. I needed time. It wasn't you. I wasn't mad. I was scared."

I searched his face. My heart thudded in my chest.

"So... what are you saying?"

He stepped closer. His voice steadied.

"I'm saying I'm sorry. For how I reacted. And that I get it

175

now."

A long beat passed between us.

Then he leaned in and kissed me.

It was slow. Tentative. Real.

I kissed him back, breath catching in my throat. My whole chest lit up.

A roar erupted outside.

We broke apart, blinking, and turned to the kitchen window.

There they were, Sarah, Greg, Sally, and half the party pressed up against the glass like spectators at a zoo exhibit. Laughing. Cheering. High-fiving. Sarah mimed wiping a tear.

"Oh my God," I groaned. "They *saw* that!"

Shawn's face turned crimson. He laughed, shaking his head. "So much for subtle."

I started laughing too, and couldn't stop. My ankle, the match, the kiss, the entire ridiculous moment, it all blended into something weirdly perfect.

For the first time in a long while, I felt... peace.

The door burst open and Sarah barreled into the kitchen, arms wide. "FINALLY!"

"Seriously?" I groaned as she hugged me.

"I've been rooting for this for *weeks*," she said, winking at Shawn. "You two are disgustingly cute."

Shawn chuckled, still pink. "I wasn't trying to make it obvious, but... apparently I suck at hiding things."

Then he turned to me. "So, think you're up for dating a college freshman?"

I smirked. "Depends on his major."

Raising an eyebrow, I asked, "And what *is* your major going to be, Mr. College Freshman?"

"Pastry school," he said, grinning. "Prepare yourself for the best desserts of your life."

I burst out laughing. "Pastry school? That's actually kind of perfect. I expect at least one honey lavender cake."

"Deal," he said, and kissed me again. Just a quick one. Another round of cheers broke out from outside. I glanced at the window. Everyone was clapping, smiling, laughing. Their joy flooded the room like sunlight.

And for once, it didn't feel like too much. It didn't overwhelm me or swallow me whole. It filled me, steady and warm, like sunlight after a long winter.

Everything had led here. Not just the match or the kiss or the party, but all of it. The hard lessons, the awkward moments, the days I wanted to give up and didn't. The people who stayed. The ones who didn't.

And still, it wasn't the end. Not even close.

This wasn't the finish line. It was the beginning of something new.

Epilogue

It was the final week of school, and the weight of finals had hit us all hard. Sarah, Shawn, and I were camped out in the library, buried under textbooks and half-finished study guides. The quiet hum of the space was a strange sort of comfort compared to the mental chaos of exam week.

Naturally, Sarah was already talking about summer classes. She flipped through a printed list like it was a vacation brochure.

"We already have homework for summer. Mrs. Kline gave us a full reading list for AP English," she said, trying to sound annoyed, though her excitement gave her away.

I groaned, chin propped up on my table. "Sarah, it's the last week of school. Can we at least *pretend* summer break exists before you ruin it?"

Shawn, sprawled out across from me like he was seconds from slipping into a coma, added, "I swear, I'm not gonna miss this place. Especially not the constant reminder that I'm a slacker."

Shawn nudged me with his foot and grinned. "But," he said, "I *am* going to miss you."

I didn't know what to say to that, so naturally, I just turned red and looked away.

That's when I heard it.

"Filler Miller and his filler crew!" Jason's voice sliced through the library like nails on a chalkboard. He strutted past with Ashley glued to his side, her face twisted into one of her usual failed glares, more constipation than threat.

I rolled my eyes. "I really hate that guy."

"Good news," Sarah chimed in, not missing a beat. "He might have to repeat the year. Ever since I stopped tutoring him, I'm pretty sure he's failing everything."

We tried not to laugh too loudly, muffling it behind books like we were in sixth grade again. It felt good, like we were finally breathing after a year of holding it all in.

As we started packing up, I slung my backpack over one shoulder. "I'll see you guys tomorrow."

Sarah blinked. "Wait, you're not coming to the Honey Hive?"

"Oh, right." I rubbed the back of my neck. "Mom wants me to head straight home. Something about the country club job."

Shawn looked mildly bummed but nodded. "Tell her we said hi. You two should come over for dinner tomorrow."

"Will do," I said, giving a lazy wave as I turned to leave.

But I didn't make it three steps before someone behind me cleared their throat.

I turned, and there was Jason.

He stood a few feet away, looking like he'd rather be anywhere else. His arms hung stiffly at his sides, his expression tight, like he was holding something in that might break him open.

"Uh... hey, Miller," he said, scratching the back of his neck. "Can I talk to you? Like... alone?"

I blinked. Jason was the last person I expected to speak to today. I glanced at Sarah and Shawn, who both shot me looks that screamed What the hell?

Still, I nodded. "Uh... yeah. Sure."

Jason led me a few shelves over, toward the back of the library, behind a row of dusty textbooks that hadn't seen daylight since the early 2000s. He leaned against the bookcase, arms crossed, avoiding my gaze.

"Okay," I said. "What's this about? Another nickname? One last shot before the year ends?"

He winced. "No. That's not." He exhaled like it physically hurt. "I wanted to apologize."

I stared. "Come again?"

"I mean it," he said, meeting my eyes. "I've been awful to you. And not just, like, normal high school jerk stuff. I was targeting you. And it wasn't fair."

I stayed quiet, not because I didn't have things to say, but because I wasn't sure what to say.

Jason shifted his weight, his eyes flicking to the floor. "The truth is... I was jealous. Of you. You were just... yourself. Open. Honest. You didn't hide, and I didn't know how to deal with that."

I frowned, unsure if I was hearing him right.

"I think I might be bi," he said, voice low. "I don't know for sure, and I've never said it out loud until now, but... yeah. And my parents?" He gave a dry laugh. "That wouldn't go over well. So when I saw you being... you, I didn't feel inspired. I felt cornered."

I swallowed hard.

Jason rubbed his hands together like they were cold. "I started dating Sarah because I thought maybe it would... I don't know... help me figure myself out. But really, I just wanted to be around you."

That hit me sideways.

"When she stopped talking about you," he added, "I started spiraling. I'd get mad at her. I'd pick fights. I couldn't explain why, but every time she defended you, it just made it worse. I wanted to know what made you so... sure of yourself."

I shook my head. "You think I'm sure of myself?"

He gave a half-smile. "You showed up every day, even when everyone was watching. I couldn't even show up to myself."

We stood in silence for a moment, the hum of fluorescent lights buzzing overhead.

"And the racket thing?" I asked quietly.

He sighed. "Ashley pushed me into it. She knew I was spiraling, and she fed into it. Said you needed to be taken down a peg, and I let her get in my head. I was pissed, confused, and I wanted to hurt someone. You were an easy target because of our history. And that's on me."

My hands clenched slightly at my sides, but I didn't speak.

"I'm not expecting you to forgive me," Jason continued. "I just needed you to hear it from me. No jokes. No sarcasm. Just... the truth."

Something about the way he said it, the weight in his voice, made it impossible to brush off.

I finally nodded. "That's a lot to carry, Jason. I hope you figure it out... for real. Not just what your parents want. Or what Ashley pushes you into."

He looked down, then back up, his eyes a little glassy. "I'm starting therapy this summer. The school counselor helped me find someone. I'm tired of being angry all the time. Especially at myself."

I took a breath, still unsure how to feel. But somewhere in the middle of it all, the edge of my anger dulled. Not because what he did was okay, but because maybe he was finally trying to fix it.

"You were a jerk," I said. "A massive jerk. But it takes guts to admit it. So... thanks."

He gave a small, unsure smile. "And I'm sorry for calling you 'Filler Miller.' That was dumb."

I smirked. "It was. But also? Weirdly catchy."

That made him laugh, actually laugh. And for the first time, he didn't look like a guy holding his breath.

As I turned to walk away, I glanced back once.

He was still standing there, in the middle of a dusty aisle, looking like someone who had just exhaled for the first time in years.

When I stepped out of the library, the afternoon sun hit me like a spotlight. Sarah and Shawn were waiting by the lockers, their faces lit up with the kind of curiosity only best friends could get away with.

"Well?" Sarah asked, practically bouncing. "What did Jason want?"

I shrugged, still sorting through the emotional dust storm. "I'll tell you later," I said, offering a tired smile. "Let's just say it wasn't what I expected."

Shawn gave me a quiet look, understanding, but not pushing. "Everything okay?"

"Yeah. I think... it will be."

We walked together toward the front of the school, our pace lazy, like none of us were quite ready to say goodbye to the year. The air held that end-of-school feeling, relief mixed with something like possibility.

"You sure you don't want to come to the Hive for one last round of celebratory lattes and pastries?" Sarah asked, nudging me.

"As tempting as that sounds," I said, "I promised my mom I'd come straight home. She wants to talk about my summer job."

"She always wants to talk about something," Sarah teased.

We paused at the curb where the buses lined up like tired beasts waiting to take us into summer. Sarah turned to me, her hand already halfway into her bag like she might pull out a clipboard.

"Let me guess," I said. "You've already made a list of summer goals?"

She grinned. "Only like three. Maybe six. Okay, nine."

I laughed. "You need help."

"Desperately."

Shawn reached out, gave my hand a quick squeeze, then let go. "Text me later?"

"Of course."

I climbed onto the bus and took my usual seat by the window. As the engine rumbled to life and the school faded behind me, I rested my head against the cool glass. My mind spun, Jason's confession, the strange hope that came with it, and the quiet thought that maybe people could change.

The ride home was short, and when I stepped through the door, Luna came bounding down the hall, tail wagging like a metronome set to joy. I dropped my bag and crouched to pet her.

"Hi, girl. Miss me?"

She barked softly, nuzzling under my hand.

"Mom?" I called out. "I'm home!"

"Living room!" she called back, and I could already hear the smile in her voice.

When I walked in, she was on the couch, phone in hand, eyes shining like she'd been holding onto a secret all afternoon.

"Okay," I said, eyeing her. "Why do you look like you just

won the lottery?"

She waved the phone. "Don't be rude, or I won't share the good news."

Mom tapped the speaker on her phone, and a voicemail began to play.

"Hi, this message is for Rion Miller, and his parent or guardian. This is Valerie James calling from the Gregory Michael Thompson Tennis Academy. I had the pleasure of watching Rion compete at the Sectional Finals last weekend."

My heart jumped. What?

"I was invited by Coach Moore, who spoke very highly of Rion and wanted me to see him in action. And I have to say, I was genuinely impressed. His grit, his focus under pressure, the way he pushed through that final set, it stood out."

I sank into the nearest chair. My brain short-circuited halfway through the message.

"We'd like to formally offer Rion a spot in our summer development program. The academy provides full scholarships to a limited number of players each year, and Rion's performance has earned him one of those slots. Tuition, travel, gear—it's all covered. He'll be training with some of the top junior players in the country."

My mouth was open, but I couldn't speak. Was this real?

The message ended with contact details and a cheerful, "We hope to hear from you soon."

Mom turned off the speaker, her eyes already glistening. "Rion?"

"Can I go?" I asked, my voice shaky and small.

She didn't even hesitate. She reached for me, pulling me into a hug, her arms tight around my back like she used to when I was little and the world felt too big to carry.

184

"Of course you can go, Rion. I'll call them first thing tomorrow."

I held on tighter than I meant to. Maybe tighter than I had in years. She didn't let go right away. I don't think either of us wanted to be the first to move.

When she finally did, she pulled back and brushed the hair from my forehead. Her voice cracked a little when she said, "Your dad would be so proud. So, so proud."

I nodded, blinking fast. "Thanks, Mom."

Then I bolted to my room.

In my room, I sat on the edge of the bed, stunned. The Gregory Michael Thompson Tennis Academy. A real shot. Something beyond our tiny town. Beyond high school courts and cafeteria milk cartons and heartbreaks and comebacks.

I let it all hit me, relief, disbelief, joy, and this soft undercurrent of fear. But the fear didn't sink me. It lifted me.

My eyes landed on the racket in the corner, still streaked with pink paint and glitter. I walked over and picked it up.

It had been vandalized. Then it carried me through the most important match of my life.

It wasn't just a racket. Not anymore.

It was proof.

That I kept going.

That I was ready.

That this was just the beginning.

ACKNOWLEDGMENTS

This book wouldn't exist without the people who patiently cheered me on, pushed me forward.

To my friends and family, you've all played a part in keeping me sane(ish) during this wild ride. Whether you offered encouragement, a sounding board, or just a "you've got this" text at the right moment, you helped me see this through.

A huge thank you to my freelance developmental editor, line editor and formatter, Sam M (highshow112@gmail.com), and my editor Diana Bright, for shaping my words with insight and patience. To my friend and cover designer, Julia Donahoe (www.juliadonahoe.com), for giving this story a face that I couldn't have dreamed up better myself.

To the brave handful of people who "unwillingly" volunteered to read countless prologues and chapters until I finally found the right tone, you are the unsung heroes of my creative chaos.

Special thanks to my earliest beta readers: Erin R., Samantha H., Jamie B., S.M. Riewe, Sierra W., and Elena R., Your thoughtful feedback, kind words, and occasional reality checks were invaluable.

And lastly, but most of all, to my husband, Dylan. Thank you for putting up with me and marathon conversations about the book, my sudden plot rants over breakfast, lunch, and dinner.

For doubling as my copy editor & proofreader (whether you wanted to or not). You've been my sounding board, and my partner in all things—and I'm endlessly grateful.

Thank You for Reading

If you've made it to this page, first of all—thank you. Thank you for spending time with this story, with these characters, and with me as a debut author. It truly means more than I can say.

If you enjoyed this book, one of the most helpful ways to support it is by leaving a quick rating or review. Even a few honest sentences about what you liked (or who you rooted for) can make a big difference in helping other readers discover the story.

You can scan the QR code to go straight to the book's Goodreads page, or you can leave a review on the site where you purchased your copy of the book.

Thank you again for reading, for caring about these characters, and for taking a moment to share your thoughts.

About the Author

Vincent Russo is an indie author making his debut with *15-Love*, a heartfelt coming-of-age story about first crushes, fierce friendships, and one unforgettable tennis season.

Vincent grew up in a small town in upstate New York and later studied Fashion Management in Boston, where he spent over a decade working in retail, e-commerce, and freelance styling. Those years taught him how much storytelling lives in the details, whether it's in clothes, visuals, or words, and that same eye for atmosphere and emotion now shapes his writing.

As a kid, Vincent didn't think of himself as much of a reader. But eventually he discovered stories that felt like escape hatches, safe spaces, and especially the LGBTQ+ romances he wished had been around when he was younger.

For more information about the author and upcoming projects, please visit vincentrussowrites.com.